International Incident

Second Edition

International Incident

Second Edition

Mike Faricy

Library of Congress Control Number: 2023915006
paperback ISBN: 978-1-962080-27-9
e-Book ISBN: 978-1-962080-28-6

MJF Publishing books may be purchased for education, Business, or promotional use. For information on bulk purchases, please contact the author directly at mikefaricyauthor@gmail.com

Published by

MJF Publishing
https://www.mikefaricybooks.com

Acknowledgments

I would like to thank the following people for their help and support:
Special thanks to my editors, Kitty, Donna and Rhonda for their hard work, cheerful patience and positive feedback.

I would like to thank Ann and Julie for their creative talent and not slitting their wrists or jumping off the high bridge when dealing with my Neanderthal computer capabilities.

Special thanks to Ann for her patience.

Last, I would like to thank family and friends for their encouragement and unqualified support. Special thanks to Maggie, Jed, Schatz, Pat, Av, Emily and Pat for not rolling their eyes, at least when I was there, and most of all, to my wife Teresa whose belief, support and inspiration has from day one, never waned.

One

I was looking forward to dinner at Heidi's. It seemed for the past couple of weeks we could never get together. Either she was busy or said she needed a night just to herself. I'd been working on an insurance fraud case and had finally put it to bed.

A guy claimed he'd been injured in a car accident. The problem was it was his third such injury in as many years. He claimed to have been rear-ended, but in all three cases, the accused drivers testified that he had backed into them as they drove down the ramp onto the interstate.

Tommy Brennan was a high school pal who now worked as an investigator for an insurance company. He caught the case about three months back, sent it my way, and it rang a bell. A little research on my part came up with a similar lawsuit from the same individual two years earlier. After backing into the other vehicle, always a senior driver, the 'victim,' Delbert Downder, would sue for twenty grand. His lawsuits carried the stipulation that if it wasn't settled quickly the cost of medical procedures, treatments and rehab could easily exceed a hundred grand. What insurance company wouldn't settle for one-fifth of that?

Anyway, with some sterling investigation on my part, Delbert Downder was charged and decided to threaten me. The end result was I'd received a nice check from the insurance company, and Downder was serving time. As a celebration, I arrived unexpectedly at Heidi's front door with two bottles of her favorite wine, rib-eye steaks, and hopes of a memorable evening.

"Hey, you're early I . . . Dev?" Was all she said when she answered the door. She wore a shocked look on her face. She stood frozen in the process of inserting a diamond earring in her left ear. Suddenly, I had the distinct feeling it hadn't been me she was expecting to see. She wore tight white slacks and a red silk top. She stared at me with wide eyes and her mouth hanging open.

"Hi, Heidi. I got your favorite wine, and your favorite steaks, and I was hoping to cook you dinner. It looks like you might have other plans. You can keep working, watch TV, or sit and talk to me. I was thinking it would be great to spend an evening and—"

"Umm, this is a really bad time. I've got a meeting tonight, and it's going to run late."

"Oh, yeah. Well, I tried to call you, but I kept on getting a recording that said you were unavailable. I couldn't even leave you a message. I just figured you might be busy, and I was hoping maybe I could help. Mind if I come in and just put this stuff in the fridge? We could get together tomorrow night or maybe the night after that. You know, whatever fits your schedule. No pressure."

She gave a quick look up and down the street and said, "Come on in for a minute. We need to talk."

We need to talk. Whenever a woman has used that phrase on me, things have never gone my way. Okay, sometimes I probably deserved it. Maybe most of the time. But not now, not tonight. I followed her into the kitchen.

Despite the fact that Heidi was possibly the worst cook in the world, the kitchen was filled with a wonderful aroma. There was a large pot on the stove and two white Styrofoam trays in the wastebasket. Two takeout meals she'd no doubt claim as her own work. The dining room table was set for two, and the candles were lit. Adele was on her sound system singing about being alone with someone.

"Oh, ahh, it looks like your meeting is here. Sorry to interrupt. I didn't know you—"

"Oh, Dev. I'm so, so sorry. I was going to tell you. I just didn't know . . ."

"It's okay, Heidi. I get it. Hey, look, you might as well keep these steaks and the wine. You know, put it to good use. Maybe your guy can fix dinner tomorrow night."

"I'm sorry, Dev. I was going to tell you. It just all happened so fast I didn't know how. Umm, can you wait just a minute? I've got something for you."

"You don't have to give me anything, Heidi. I'm just sorry. I shouldn't have come over without—"

"Here," she said, opening the pantry closet. She handed me a cardboard box for twelve bottles of wine. Only it held two plastic paint trays, my paint roller, and a couple of brushes. As I took the box, she reached back into the pantry and grabbed a brown paper grocery bag by the handles, and handed it to me. Boxers, a couple of t-shirts, some socks, my St. Paul Saints sweatshirt and a pair of my running shoes.

"Oh yeah, thanks. This is great. I've been looking for this stuff."

"Oh, Dev."

"No, really. Don't worry about it, Heidi. We're both adults. I wish you all the best. I better get out of here before your guest arrives." I made a beeline for the front door. Carrying the wine box and the grocery bag, I turned and pushed the screen door handle using my hip. I looked at Heidi, gave her a wink and a smile, and made tracks to my car before she saw the tears.

I tossed the cardboard box and the grocery bag into the back seat of my car, a '91 Ford Escort. The driver's door was taped closed so it wouldn't fall off. I had to open the front passenger door and slide over the console into the driver's seat. The car started on the third try, and I headed down the street. Just as I got to the corner, a red Lexus LC came around the corner and headed up the street. It was an expensive, sporty looking thing with a large chrome grill. I watched in the rearview mirror as it came to a stop right in front of Heidi's house. A moment later, some guy wearing a dark suit and open-collared shirt climbed out. He reached back into the car and grabbed a bouquet of white flowers. Probably roses. He waved toward the house, which suggested Heidi was still standing at the door, watching. It looked like she'd done pretty well for herself.

TWO

Three weeks later.

"No. You're not listening, sweetheart. Now, I want you to stay right here in bed. I'm going to make you breakfast, and then I'm going to bring it into you. We'll have breakfast in bed, and, well, who knows what might happen after that. Now sit up for a second."

Maddie had just finished law school. Her hair was dyed yellow, not blonde, but a bright yellow that faded into green for the last inch or two. It was all kinky curls and hung down to her shoulders. She wrinkled her nose and gave me a kiss. As I sat up, she pulled her pillow on top of mine and sort of fluffed them up before gently pushing me back. She gave me a quick peck on the cheek and rolled out of bed. She searched around on the floor before she found her thong and pulled it on.

The thong was red with a cut out in the shape of a heart in the front. She stepped over to the nightstand on her side of the bed, picked up the TV remote, and tossed it over to me. "Here Dev, you can watch the news. I'll be back with breakfast in five minutes. Don't go any-where," she giggled and wrinkled her nose again.

I wanted to pull her back into bed. "You sure I can't give you a hand?"

"No, it will be a lot better if you stay right there. This will only take a couple of minutes."

"Don't take any longer than that. I'm missing you already."

She giggled, grabbed her cellphone, and began texting as she strutted out of the room.

I didn't feel like watching the news. It was more like twenty-five minutes before she returned. She was carrying a large wooden tray with two plates and two mugs of coffee. Both plates featured a stack of three pancakes drowning in an ocean of syrup and three sausages. Her eyes were focused on the tray, walking slowly, taking tiny steps as she came around to my side of the bed.

"Here can you take this?" She said, placing the tray on my lap. The coffee mugs were literally filled to the brim, and as she set the tray down, a wave of steaming coffee rolled over the side of both mugs and onto the tray. She seemed not to notice, hurried around the bed, and climbed in on her side.

We'd had three dates over the past two weeks. Last night, following another party, we came back to her apartment for, *'A little glass of wine.'* We never had the wine. In fact, I'm not even sure she had any wine in her apartment. Not a complaint, by the way.

Along with the yellow-green hair she had deep brown eyes and a lacy little tattoo on her tail bone that read 'Welcome'. I didn't bother to comment.

"Okay, dig in," she said.

I carefully handed a plate over to her, followed by a knife and fork. She sat next to me with her legs crossed, and the plate balanced on her lap. "Say, would you mind turning that cartoon off? It's kind of distracting, and it's starting to give me a headache."

I clicked off the TV and tossed the remote on the bed. "You sure the headache isn't from the margaritas you were drinking last night."

"Mmm-mmm, that too, probably," she said and stuffed some pancakes into her mouth.

I cut a wedge from my stack of pancakes, took a bite, and almost got sick. The things tasted burnt.

Maddie reached for her coffee mug, and as she took a sip, I lifted the top pancake on my stack. The one in the middle was blackened, and the bottom one looked charred.

"How's the breakfast?"

"Umm, good, Maddie. Very good. What's not to like about breakfast in bed?" I stabbed one of the sausages with my fork and cut off a bite. It was cold. Not cold like it had been out of the pan too long, but cold, as in nearly frozen. It sort of crunched as I bit into it.

Maddie placed her plate on the nightstand next to the bed, apparently finished after two bites. She held her coffee mug in one hand, her cell phone in the other, and wore a big smile. I was focused on her little red thong. "Good?" She asked, not bothering to look up. She was sending a text to someone using just one thumb to quickly crank out the message.

"Delicious," I replied. I took the tray and carefully set it on top of the chest of drawers on my side of the bed. I took hold of the coffee mug, settled back on the two pillows, and took a sip as I faced her. It was instant coffee, lukewarm instant coffee.

"That's all you're eating?" She said, scrolling through messages.

"I can eat, or I can sit here and study how beautiful you are."

She smiled, set her mug on the nightstand next to her plate, and curled up next to me. "Everyone was right. You are full of shit. But that was sort of sweet. You know, I'm going on that trip to Paris right after my graduation ceremony. I just wanted to let you know I'm really going to miss you." She went back to texting, this time using both thumbs.

"Well, if it makes you feel any better, I'm going to miss you, too. But you'll love Paris. Have you ever been?"

"To Paris? No, I've only been out of the country twice, both times fishing in Canada with my dad and brothers. I've been to California and Florida, but this will be my first time to Paris. I can't wait. You sure you can't come?"

I took that as a compliment. We chatted for another minute or two. Maddie suddenly raised her eyebrows and climbed on top of me. Just as it seemed to be getting very interesting, her cellphone signaled a text coming through. She continued to move rhythmically, reached for her phone, and proceeded to send a reply. Apparently, she was a master at double-tasking. After a replay of our late night activity, she told me she had to get ready for a meeting. I got dressed and headed out the door. On my way past the kitchen, I happened to notice the package of frozen pancakes next to the toaster and the sausage package next to the microwave.

Three

I left Maddie's a little before nine. It turned out her luncheon meeting was with an uncle. She actually referred to him as her favorite uncle. She was going to do some sort of pro bono work for him since he had apparently paid her law school tuition. I wasn't sure she really grasped just how wonderful he was to do that for her. I made a mental note to try and meet him in the near future.

As I pulled in front of my house, I saw Morton standing on the couch, looking out the window. He began barking as I slid across the console and stepped out of the passenger side of the car. Morton met me at the front door. No sooner had I stepped inside the house than he literally ran to the back door, barking all the way. Morton's translation probably would have been something along the lines of, "It's about time." I barely opened the back door before he shot across the porch and into the yard. He spun around in a circle a couple of times and assumed the position, all the while giving me a disgusted look.

After the midnight and morning workout with Maddie, not to mention no breakfast, I was starving. I scrambled a half dozen eggs, made some toast, and put on a pot of real coffee. Morton and I had breakfast together, I showered, and we headed down to the office.

My officemate, Louie Laufen, was sitting at his desk, actually a picnic table, when we arrived. The table was covered with a number of files. Louie was leaning back in his chair with his feet up on the table. He was on his phone, and he gave me a nod as we entered. Morton headed toward his bed in front of the file cabinet, and I opened the second drawer on my desk, pulled out my binoculars, and scanned the apartment building across the street. Louie finished his phone conversation just as I finished scanning the apartment windows across the street.

"Hey, Dev. Any luck?"

"No, it's already after ten. Everyone's already gone off to work."

"Actually, I meant your date last night."

"Oh, yeah, had a really great evening. Yet another party of folks she said she went to law school with. Not that anyone wanted to talk about it. I didn't know any of them, and once they found out what I do for a living, they weren't interested in knowing anything more about me."

"Yeah, it'll be party time for all of them for about a week. But believe me that damn bar exam is already hanging over their heads. Some of them will try and take the exam in July, but if they're anything like my class, the vast majority will be shooting for February. Sounds like a long way off, but in short order, the damn thing is here. You know when this Patty is looking to take it?"

"Patty dumped me a couple of months ago. This girl is Maddie, Louie, and no, she hasn't mentioned the bar exam. She had to hurry and get ready for a meeting this morning. She's going to be doing some pro bono stuff for her uncle. Get this. The guy paid her law school tuition."

"Her uncle paid her tuition? That's a good chunk of change and an awfully nice thing to do. Does he have some big company or somewhere she's going to be working at?"

"I don't know. She never really mentioned him before. She didn't actually say much except that he paid her tuition. Anyway, that's why we had to cut things short this morning. She has a luncheon meeting with him today. In fact, she's probably heading there right about now."

"What'd you say his name was?"

"I didn't. She never told me, and with the exception of this morning when she kicked me out of her bed, I can't recall another time she's ever mentioned him. Probably some guy into high tech internet stuff, or a doctor, or something."

"Or maybe he's a judge or practices himself. You ever find out who he is, let me know. At the end of the day, it's still a pretty small community, and I can maybe give you an update on the guy."

"We'll see what develops. We've only gone out a couple of times."

"Which is probably why she's still interested in you. Wait until she gets to know you a little better, she'll run screaming for the nearest exit."

Four

Louie left the office for a court appearance around two that afternoon, another DUI case. Driving Under the Influence. If you were arrested for driving under the influence in this town, Louie Laufen was the guy you wanted to represent you. He'd become Mister DUI in the city, not that he'd ever been arrested for it. Well, actually, he had been once, but he got off on a technicality, so it never appeared on his record.

I had a cop pal who told me once that most people, after a couple of drinks, think, 'I better wait for a while and not have another drink before I head home.' But if you've had seven or eight drinks, you're probably going to order one more for the road and figure you're okay to drive.

Louie said the guy he was representing had been arrested twice before in the past three years. The best scenario was going to be jail time, a revoked license, and a substantial fine. That was before they increased his car insurance if he could even get insurance. Jail for one to three years and car insurance for about a grand a month for the next ten years after that was a hell of a price to pay for being stupid about drinking.

After Louie left, I took Morton for a quick walk around the block. I deposited the dog poop bag in the trash can in front of my building and headed back up to the office. Morton sat in front of my desk, waiting for the dog biscuit he always got after our afternoon walk. Once I tossed him the biscuit, he lost all interest in me and headed over to his bed alongside the file cabinet. I grabbed the binoculars and did an early scan of the apartment building across the street. Nothing shaking.

I was about to replace the binoculars in my desk when a car pulled up and parked across the street right behind my Ford Escort. It was a large SUV, a black Cadillac Escalade to be specific. It wasn't the chrome spinning wheel hubcaps, or the windows tinted darker than the law allowed that caught my attention. Unpleasant experiences began to flood my memory. When the driver's door opened, a massive male figure oozed out of the seat and looked up at me, staring out the window. All my hopes were dashed, and it was already too late to hide.

Fat Freddy Zimmerman saw me and flashed me the finger as he walked around to the passenger side of the Escalade. Along the way, he spit on the trunk of my car. He opened the rear passenger door for his boss, local crime lord Tubby Gustafson. Tubby appeared to groan as he slid out of the back seat, and the large car rocked from side to side. He stepped onto the sidewalk and took a moment to adjust his tie.

Fat Freddy appeared to whisper something to him. Tubby glanced up at me, staring down at the two of them. He gave me the finger as he proceeded to cross the street and headed for the door to my building. Great minds think alike.

A car sped down the street and had to slam on the brakes to avoid hitting Fat Freddy and Tubby. Thankfully, the driver didn't honk. Instead, he just nodded politely when Freddy gave him a look. They disappeared from sight, and a moment later, I heard the staircase begin to creak. I listened to the two of them groan and wheeze as they headed up the stairs. I hoped somehow Freddy and Tubby might be headed for an appointment at the hairdressers just across the hall from me. No such luck. All was quiet for a few seconds until a red-faced Fat Freddy held the door to my office open, and the city's crime lord, Tubby Gustafson, stepped in.

He had a look on his face, more disgusted than usual, as he glanced around the office. He shook his head, waddled up to my desk and waited for Freddy to pull the client chair out.

Morton looked up and apparently recognized all six hundred plus pounds Tubby and Fat Freddy brought to the table. He simply lowered his head and placed his paws over his eyes. Who could blame him? Tubby glared at me with cold blue eyes. His nose, the size of a baked potato, was red and pocked marked. It looked as if someone with football spikes had stomped on it a couple of times.

"Apparently, some things never seem to change," Tubby said, as he settled into the client chair. The chair creaked, suggesting it might break into kindling at any moment. He indicated the binoculars I was still holding with a wiggle of his chins. I quickly placed the binoculars into an open desk drawer and pushed it closed with my knee. "I see you've done absolutely nothing along the lines of sprucing up this dump. Sit down, Haskell. You're making me nervous standing there, pretending to think. Does it hurt?"

I didn't answer his question. "To what do I owe the pleasure of a visit, Tub . . . er, umm, Mister Gustafson?"

"Oh, please. Spare me the attempt at manners. I have a bone to pick with you."

"Me? What have I . . . Mister Gustafson I haven't seen you for the better part of a month, possibly two. I've been investigating people for the past three weeks for an insurance company. Just making sure their resumes and employment applications are correct. I've been involved in nothing on the criminal end of things. Not that I consider you a criminal, sir. I haven't talked to the police or federal authorities, and I certainly haven't mentioned your name to anyone else." Why bother, I thought.

"Collateral damage, Haskell."

"Excuse me?"

"Get your head out of your ass and listen up."

"Oh, I heard you, sir. It just isn't making any sense."

"No doubt because you make such a damn mess of everything you touch. After a while, I'm sure it all just runs together for an idiot of your ilk."

"Maybe if you gave me a clue, sir."

"A clue? How about the name Madeline Swanson."

Jesus Christ, Maddie? My late night erotic cuddle? Breakfast in bed Maddie? Maddie in the red thong with the perfectly placed heart cutout? Maddie with the welcome sign tattooed just above her gorgeous rear end? Maddie with the yellow and green hair? "Madeline Swanson, sir?"

"Don't play stupid with me, Haskell. You're so damn stupid you can't even play stupid well. Yes, Madeline Swanson. My niece, by the way."

Shit. "Well, I know a Madeline Swanson, a law school student. I mean, she was a student. She just finished law school. As a matter of fact, she's graduating with honors. This weekend."

"She is graduating Summa Cum Laude. Do you even know what that means, Haskell?"

"Umm, that she's really brilliant?"

"It means that she's too good for the likes of you and your contemporaries. Now, after all her hard work and my investment, the poor thing has unwittingly presented me with a problem."

"A problem, sir?"

"Yes, you dunderhead. A very big problem. Namely you."

"Oh, sorry sir. I didn't know. I mean, maybe if I explained to her that we're acquainted perhaps that would, umm, help to eliminate the problem."

"Acquainted? You're missing the point, as always. I don't want the likes of you to have anything at all to do with my niece."

"You mean, we should stop seeing one another?"

"Good Lord. If only it was that easy. No, Haskell, that's too damn abrupt. You're going to let her down easy. Do you understand?"

"Down easy. Yes, sir."

"Now, she's graduating at the weekend after which she's off to Paris for some sightseeing."

"I knew about her trip. I mean, she told me she was going. That will be the perfect time for her to get me out of her mind and I can pretend to be busy when she gets back to town and—"

"Silencio, you moron. You'll do no such thing. I'm sending you to Paris on the same flight. You'll act as her bodyguard for the week. This will be perfect. You can report to me every day. Give me an update on her activities. God forbid she'd actually meet someone nice over there," he said and looked me up and down.

"Paris, Mister Gustafson?"

"Yes. Have you ever been?"

"No, sir."

"I don't suppose you speak French?"

"No, sir."

"Even better. You'll just follow her around and not get in the way. I'll be booking you a separate room in her hotel. Other than carrying her luggage, you're not to touch her or anything belonging to her. Do I make myself clear?"

"Yes, sir. But, Paris? I mean, are you sure? I've got work lined up and I—"

"Haskell, please do not present me with one more problem. Work lined up? Maybe instead of a week in Paris, you'd prefer a two week stay in a hospital, in traction. Do I make myself clear?" He paused for a moment before shouting, "Well, do I?"

"Yes, sir. Very clear."

"One other thing. You are forbidden to attend her graduation ceremony or the reception that follows. She's worked damn hard, and I'm not about to have the likes of you ruin the event. Should you decide to show, you won't live to see the sunset. Questions?

"No sir, understood."

"God, the things I do. Come along, Freddy. Get me out of here before I follow my instincts and eliminate Haskell as a problem once and for all. And Haskell, God help you if you even think of mentioning this conversion to Madeline. I find out you so much as mentioned this to her, and we can skip the hospital stay and focus on a paupers grave. Capiche?"

Fat Freddy pulled the chair back as Tubby stood. He walked to the door, turned, and looked like he was about to say something. After a long moment, he simply shook his head and growled, "Oh, what in the hell is the point?"

Fat Freddy followed him out the door and down the stairs. I watched from the window, waiting for the two of them to exit the building and appear on the street be-low. Tubby stepped off the curb in front of the bus that was pulling over to pick up two passengers. The driver slammed on the brakes but didn't honk the horn. Fat Freddy hurried across the street and held the rear passenger door open for Tubby. He closed the door once Tubby settled in. He looked up at me staring out the window and gave me the finger again before he climbed in behind the wheel. The tinted windows were so dark that once the doors were closed I couldn't see either one of them. A moment later, the Escalade was racing up the hill. I stood and watched out the window until it disappeared from sight.

Five

It was after four when Louie came back to the office. "Jesus, who died?" He said, having taken no more than two steps into the office.

"My latest romance just went down the tubes compliments of Tubby Gustafson."

"Tubby Gustafson is dating that chick?"

"No, he's not dating Maddie. It's even worse. He's her uncle."

"Oh, family."

"Yeah, turns out he's the benevolent uncle who picked up the tab on her law school tuition."

"How'd you find this out?"

"You kidding? His fat ass was here, not thirty minutes ago. Get this, he threatened me about a dozen different ways, and after all that, he tells me I have to go with her on a trip to Paris and act as a bodyguard."

"Paris, Texas?"

"No, Louie. Paris. The Paris. The Paris in France."

"And this is a problem?"

"Yeah. Well, I mean, he wants me to dump her. I'm supposed to stay in a separate room. And I have to keep her safe."

"Keep her . . . What is she going to be doing over there that you need to keep her safe?" Louie tossed his briefcase on his picnic table desk, sat down in his desk chair, and rolled it over to the little refrigerator we have in the corner. He opened the door and pulled a beer out. "You want one."

"Think it would help?"

"Can't hurt," he said and tossed the can over to me.

I popped the top on the can, and beer sprayed across my desk. "Oh, man, can you believe it."

We finished the beers, had two more, and two more after that. Louie opened the refrigerator again and peered inside. "Why does this always happen? We're out."

"Out of beer?"

"No Dev, we're out of fine wine. Yes, beer. Come on, let's go over to The Spot. I'll even get the first round. Besides, poor Morton looks like he could use a bag of pork rinds."

Mike was tending bar, and we grabbed a couple of stools in the corner. Morton was next to Louie, waiting patiently for the next pork rind to be handed to him. Louie had already eaten half the bag.

"And you're leaving next Tuesday?" Louie said.

"Yeah. Maddie graduates over the weekend, has Monday to pack, and her flight's on Tuesday. Well, I guess now it's our flight."

"And Tubby is buying you a ticket and paying for your hotel room?"

"That's what he said."

"Sounds nuts to me. Let me see if I got this straight. Tubby tells you to stay away from his niece, and the next thing he does is turn around and buy you a ticket on the same flight. He books you a room in the same hotel? That sounds crazy."

"Yeah, well, he's booking me a different room."

"So don't stay in it. If he's picking up the tab, what do you care if you don't use it? Not like it's costing you anything."

"Yeah, but Tubby—"

"Dev, Tubby's not going to be there. Tubby is going to be over here. Thousands of miles away. All you have to do is call him every day and tell him everything is fine. He's not going to know the difference. You can enjoy yourself, have a great time, and break up with her on the flight home."

"Sounds like a real jerk move."

"Yeah, so?"

"So, I don't want to do that." I signaled Mike for two more beers just as the front door opened, and a guy I knew walked in. He scanned the room, focused on Louie and me, and headed in our direction.

"Hey, hi, Dev. I was hoping I'd find you in here."

"Hi, Matt. We're kind of in a business meeting right now." I indicated Louie with a nod of my head.

"Yeah, yeah, sorry to interrupt, but I've been look-ing for you."

"Looking for me? No offense, but if I remember correctly, you still owe me for the last time I helped you out. Remember? The guy who set you up on the jewelry heist. What was his name?"

"Not important, besides he's still in jail. But that's why I've been looking for you. I wanted to pay you, and I've even added interest."

"You're kidding?"

"No, really, I'm serious, man." He took out a wallet from his back pocket, pulled a check out of the wallet, and handed it to me one thousand dollars with today's date. "I added a hundred bucks in interest," he said.

"That's very kind of you, Matt." I glanced at the check, Matteo Martin. "What's with the Matteo? I thought your name was Matthew."

"Same thing, just in French."

"French? Your last name is Martin."

"Yeah, happens to be the most popular last name in France. Sort of like Smith over here."

"You're kidding me?"

"No, both my folks came over as college students and settled here."

"You mean, you're French?"

"Well, American, born and raised, but yeah, my folks are from Paris."

"Paris? I gotta go over there in about a week. You want a beer?"

Six

Maddie's graduation ceremony was at two on Sunday afternoon. I never received an invitation, but I Googled the event. It was held in the Minneapolis Convention center, Room 101. The graduates would receive their Juris Doctor degrees, and everyone had to sit and listen to some judge's speech. Tubby's reception for Maddie immediately followed the ceremony and was going to be at the Centerfold Cabaret, one of his establishments. Kind of strange that her graduation reception was held at a strip club, but then again, Tubby was the host. I took his threat forbidding me to attend either event upon penalty of death as legit. I told Maddie I couldn't make it because I was investigating an inside robbery job and wouldn't be free until later that night. She didn't sound like she bought my excuse when she gave her reply.

"Fine. Whatever."

"Oh, glad you could finally make it," she said, not sounding like she meant a word as she opened her apartment door late Sunday evening. She was wearing a skimpy bikini and took a hearty sip of a pink liquid in a stemmed glass. No kiss, no handshake, not even so much as a wink. She simply turned, pranced back into her living room, and set the glass on an end table. She stood in front of a full-length oval mirror I recognized as having come from her bedroom and began to dance to some music I didn't recognize. She faced sideways with her hands above her head, studying her figure in the mirror as she danced. She turned after a couple of minutes and repeated the process studying her opposite side. Surprisingly, she was really good. I figured she must have caught sight of a couple of the girls onstage while attending her reception at the Centerfold Cabaret. Eventually, she stopped and turned down the music. She flopped onto the couch, grabbed her stemmed glass, and drained it.

"Whew, what a workout. That's some tough competition."

"What?"

"Oh, umm, the dancers I saw at my reception."

"Your reception at the Centerfold Cabaret? Your uncle's place. You had strippers in there?"

"First of all, we're . . . I mean, they're not called strippers. They're called dancers, Mister Know It All. And third, for your information, my reception happened to be held in a very private room upstairs with mirrors on all the walls and very comfortable chairs."

"I'll bet."

"And just what is that supposed to mean."

"Nothing, Maddie. I'm glad you had a lovely reception and congratulations on earning a law degree, not to mention being at the top in your class. That's quite an accomplishment. You should—"

"Course, when you're not wearing anything that makes a big difference," she said, looking down at the bikini barely covering her.

"What?"

"The dancers, Dev. God, if you're doing that every day you have to be in great shape. I was thinking. Oh, hey, get me another, will you? Shaker's on the kitchen counter," she said and handed me her empty glass. "I was thinking, you know, working out every day for an hour or two and getting paid for it. It kind of makes sense."

I came back from the kitchen with her refilled glass as she stood in front of the mirror, shaking her upper body from side to side. Her beverage consumption seemed to be taking effect. "Umm, thanks," she said and took another healthy sip.

"Was your uncle at the reception?"

"Of course he was. He owns the place. It's one more civic thing he does. He helps all the dancers earn money so they can continue their academic studies."

"Their studies?"

"Hello. A lot of people don't know this, but he only hires medical students. Not only do they get daily exercise, but they can study human anatomy at the same time. He told me his graduation rate was over ninety percent."

"His graduation rate is over ninety percent? Gee, imagine. Hey, Maddie, here I brought you a little gift. I meant what I said earlier, congratulations on graduating.

That's really impressive." I handed her the gift-wrapped picture frame I'd picked up on the way over.

"Mmm-mmm, yeah, thanks," she said. She took the present, tossed it on the couch, and positioned herself in front of the mirror. She slowly spread her legs and proceeded to do the splits. She made it all the way down and held the position while she turned from side to side.

"I'm really sorry I had to work," I lied. "Just comes with the job, I'm afraid."

"That's okay. I only worked my ass off for a bunch of years to get this far."

I thought it best not to reply.

She turned on the music, stood with her back to the mirror, and studied her reflection over her right shoulder. "God, does my ass look fat? I need to tone up so I'd get more tips, umm, if I was dancing. She plopped down on the couch and drained half her glass. Five minutes later, her head was leaning back, resting on the couch. Her mouth was open, and she was snoring. Loudly.

I turned off the dreadful music, grabbed a blanket from her bedroom, and covered her up. I dumped the contents of her glass down the sink. I did the same with the remnants in the stainless steel drink shaker and placed everything in the dishwasher. I filled a glass with water, took two aspirin from the medicine cabinet in the bathroom, and placed them on the coffee table in front of the couch. I shook my head, considering another failed opportunity, let myself out and headed home.

Morton was asleep on the living room couch when I stepped into the house. He didn't move when I opened the front door, and he didn't move when I closed the door. After the third time I called his name, he opened one eye.

"Hey, Morton, come on. Let's go outside. Come on, Morton. Outside. Outside."

Gradually, it dawned on him, I wasn't going to go away. He slowly rose, hopped down on the floor, and stretched. While he stretched, he studied me before finally making his way to the back door.

"Good boy, come on, outside. Let's go outside. Come on, Morton." He was back at the door in about ninety seconds. When I let him in, he ignored me and headed upstairs. I drank a glass of water, brushed my teeth, and wandered into the bedroom. Morton was already snoring softly. I climbed into bed and turned on the TV.

Seven

Having gone to bed early, Morton decided it was time for both of us to get up just after five the following morning. Actually, it wasn't that much of a problem. I was wide awake, dreading tomorrow's flight to Paris. We were in the office a little after seven. Louie walked in around ten. I was on the phone, counting the number of times it rang before Maddie answered. Eventually, I got dumped into her voice mail.

"What the hell time did you get in this morning?" Louie said as he emptied the last of the coffee into his barely half-full mug.

"Oh, I had the day from hell yesterday." I went on to remind him about Tubby forbidding me to go to Maddie's graduation and her reception. I told him about Maddie in her bikini, making a bunch of stripper moves, and just when I was thinking the night was going to be memorable, she passed out on the couch.

"Okay, no offense, Dev, but maybe all of that was a good thing."

"She's not talking to me. She's mad as hell I didn't go to her graduation and reception. Stop me when we get to the good part."

"Well, for starters, her uncle, Tubby Gustafson, didn't have you killed. He wants you to nicely dump her while acting as her bodyguard over the course of the next week. By the way, have you started to pack yet?"

"I was going to do that tomorrow."

"Tomorrow?"

"He told me the flight is scheduled to take off at ten minutes to five. I'll have more than enough time."

"You got anything your working on I should know about?"

"No, just those insurance company job applications, and I'm a week ahead, so I'm cool."

"You give a thought to what you're going to do with the brains of the outfit?"

"I gave him a look. "Who are you talking about?"

"Morton."

"Oh, man, I guess I sort of forgot about him. Think I could bring him with?"

"No, you've got to have all sorts of things lined up in advance to get through customs, and you don't. So, no. Tell you what, how about he stays with me?"

"Really? You'd do that for me?"

"No, but I'd do it for Morton. Besides, having him spend every day in the office will at least provide some sense of normality, whatever that is in his life."

"That'd be great, Louie."

"Good, bring his food and water dishes along with a bag of dog food tomorrow morning, and I'll give you a ride out to the airport. You probably should be out there no later than two-thirty.”

“Two-thirty?”

“Here’s the deal, if you get out there early, you’ll no doubt sail through the TSA lines in about ten minutes. If you put yourself on a tight schedule, you’ll end up in some line that never moves. You tell Maddie you’re going yet?”

I shook my head. “Far as I know, she’s unaware unless Tubby told her. I planned to tell her last night, but she wasn’t interested in anything I had to say. Plus, she was sipping some pink drink and ended up falling asleep on the couch. I left her some aspirin and a glass of water, covered her up, and went home. So much for my plans for a fun-filled night.”

“I feel your pain, man, but let’s be honest. That’s nothing compared to what’s going to happen if you get on the wrong side of Tubby. Just do yourself a favor, look at this next week as strictly business. You’re her bodyguard. And by the way, she doesn’t need one. Tubby’s paying the bill. Take a week off. Be professional for once, and at the end of the week, you two go your separate ways. Problem solved.”

“But I like her. A lot.”

“Yeah, and you liked Heidi, and Patty, and Molly, and Chrissy and . . .”

“Okay, okay. You made your point.”

“Hopefully,” Louie said.

Eight

On Tuesday morning, Morton and I made it into the office just before noon. I stopped and picked up an extra-large pizza with everything on it and double cheese, Louie's favorite.

"Well, good morning. It's about time. I was beginning to wonder," Louie said.

"Yeah, I packed, took Morton for a long walk, and got us a little something special. Pizza, double cheese with everything on it."

"Oh, you are the best, Dev. Now, I'm not trying to bug you, but you got your passport?"

I patted my right front pocket.

"Cash?"

"Yeah, dollars. I'll change them into euros at the Paris airport."

"Boarding pass?"

"I've got a reservation number. I have to input that at the kiosk, and they'll print it off."

"Luggage?"

"Tossed it in your car."

"Positive attitude?"

"It's getting there."

"Then let's have some lunch," Louie said and opened the pizza box I set on his picnic table. He looked for the largest piece and took it. "Mmm-mmm, this is great, man," he said through a pizza filled mouth. Louie had pretty much inhaled that first piece before I even pulled a chair over. He tossed his crust back into the box.

The pizza was cut into eight slices. Louie ate six of them. Actually, I had butterflies in my stomach thinking about the flight, worrying about Maddie, and all the while thinking about pain in the ass Tubby lurking in the background. I didn't know what to expect. I stayed focused on the fact that, once I made it through airport security, I was free from Fat Freddy Zimmerman and Tubby Gustafson. That was all the incentive I needed. We sat and chatted while Louie finished all six pieces of pizza. I, slowly, began to calm down a little.

"Well," Louie said, looking at his watch. "Why don't we head out there. Better to cool your heels once you're through security instead of pacing back and forth in here."

"Who's pacing?"

"You know what I mean. Besides, we get there a little early there's a better chance you won't run into Tubby."

"You think he'll be there?"

"Maybe, maybe not. But why take the chance? He's not flying so they won't let him through security. It'll maybe give you some time to smooth things over with this Maddie girl. Just remember, you're going to nicely, politely, bring this relationship to a close before it even gets off the ground.”

“Yeah, yeah, I get it. Come on, let’s get a move on before you think of something else to lecture me about.”

We made it out to the airport in record time, barely fifteen minutes. Louie pulled up in front of the very last departure gate and stopped. He was two lanes over and blocking traffic. Horns immediately started honking behind us.

“Sounds like a lot of people are anxious to see you leave town. Better hurry and get out, Dev.”

“Thanks, Louie, appreciate the ride out here, and thanks for looking after Morton. Morton, you behave now. Be a good boy, and I’ll see you in a week.” Someone behind us leaned on the horn for a long blast.

Louie jumped at a sudden knock on his window. A cop wearing a green high visibility vest said, “Sir, either move this vehicle now, or I’ll have you towed.”

“You heard the man, Dev.”

I scratched Morton behind the ear, grabbed my suitcase from the back seat, and hurried across two lanes of parked cars toward the terminal door. Once out of the street and on the sidewalk, I turned to give a final wave to Louie, but his car had already disappeared. A long line of cars began to follow him down the exit. A nondescript black Toyota with an elderly couple that looked to be in their eighties rolled past. The woman looked at me, glared, and gave me the finger before they disappeared around the corner.

Nine

It pained me to think about it, but Louie had been right. With plenty of time to sit around in the airport, I cleared TSA in less than fifteen minutes. My flight was departing from the last gate at the very end of the mile-long concourse. I could have taken a train to the gate, but I decided to stroll. My appetite had returned, and I stopped at a McDonalds, paid double the usual price for lunch, and carried the bag to my gate.

I arrived at my gate almost two and a half hours before the flight was scheduled for departure, sat down, and tried to figure out what I was going to tell Maddie. Occasionally a fellow passenger drifted into the area. Over the next half hour, that gradually grew to a stream. I was just about to open my second cheeseburger when a voice whispered in my ear, "Wake the hell up, dumb shit, and pay attention."

I looked over my shoulder. Fat Freddy Zimmerman sat in the chair behind me, grinning.

"Freddy?"

"Way to be on top of things. Come on. Someone would like to talk to you."

"Where are we going?"

"You're going to follow me. Now, come on, get your ass in gear."

"Hey, man. I got a flight to catch."

"Well, then you better get your dumb ass in gear. Here, let me carry that for you," he said, glancing at my McDonalds bag.

"That's all right. I got it."

"Not making a very good impression."

"Okay, okay. Here, but don't eat any of it."

"Don't worry, I won't," he said and headed back up the concourse.

"I looked around to see if any other of Tubby's thugs were nearby. If they were, Tubby had apparently started hiring senior citizens. I followed two steps behind Fat Freddy and constantly checked around me to see if any unsavory types had joined us. As we passed the screens listing departures, Freddy took my McDonalds bag and tossed it into a trash bin.

"Hey, Freddy. What the hell are you doing? I wasn't finished with that."

"Too late now, besides it was empty," he said and swallowed the last of my cheeseburger.

The Runway was an airport bar just next to the men's room. Fat Freddy headed into the bar. He had to turn sideways to squeeze past the various folks sitting on bar stools. He sidestepped to the end of the bar and headed for a distant corner. As I came around the end of the bar, I glanced ahead and there, seated at the corner table with his back to the wall sat Tubby Gustafson. Not so surprisingly, no one was sitting at the table next to him. Fat Freddy turned, pointed at me, and indicated the chair opposite Tubby with a nod. I sat down across the table from Tubby. Freddy stood behind me, effectively blocking any customer's view of our interaction along with all the sunlight.

Tubby held a glass with about a quarter-inch of what looked like whiskey. He took a sip and stared at me for a long moment. "Amazing, you're here with time to spare."

"I didn't want to miss the flight."

"Have you spoken to Madeline?"

"You told me not to."

"That wasn't my question. Always a problem, Haskell. Always making it difficult. I'm going to try again, so listen carefully. Have you spoken to Madeline."

"No, sir."

"She'll be at the gate when you return. She's checked her bag. It's heavy. I want you to get it for her at baggage claim in Paris and bring it to her hotel room."

"Okay, but I've checked my own bag so I—"

"Oh please. That worn black thing with the duct tape? Nothing like a first impression. God, you'll be lucky if they even load it on the plane." He waited for a response, and when I didn't reply, he said, "Against my better judgment, I'll expect you to take her to dinner. I'll want to know where and when in advance. Hours in advance."

"No offense, Mister Gustafson, but didn't you basically tell me not to get involved with her. I think you told me not to talk to her. To stay in my room. To simply act as a bodyguard and not to—"

"Believe me. I know what I said. You may take her to dinner. However a word of advice, look but do not touch. Clear?"

"Yes, sir, very."

"Perfect," he said and handed a number ten business envelope to me. "I'll expect you to take her someplace nice. Now, remember, you are to carry her suitcase at all times unless it is secured in her hotel room. Any questions?"

"No, sir."

"All right. You will remain here, at this table, for another two minutes. What that means Haskell is you count to ten. You can count to ten, can't you?"

"Yeah, I think so," I joked.

"The day is full of surprises. Count to ten six times, slowly. That will be sixty seconds, and that makes up one whole minute. Once you've finished, do it again."

"I'll try and remember that, sir."

He didn't laugh. "Remain here for two minutes, Haskell," Tubby said. He stood and brushed past me, actually bumping my chair sideways as he went by. I noticed as he passed that he wore what looked like a TSA badge clipped to the bottom of his suit coat.

While I waited for the prescribed minute, I quickly opened up the envelope he'd handed me. I fanned through the cash and counted one hundred and fifty euros. In an effort to not follow his instructions, I stood and left the table. I stepped out of the Runway Bar and glanced up the concourse just in time to see Tubby and Fat Freddy entering a door labeled Airport Personnel Only.

Ten

Just about all of the seats were now taken at the gate area. I scanned the room and saw Maddie sitting at the far end of a row reading something on her cell-phone. She had a pair of earbuds plugged into her ears.

I walked down the row, stepping around various pieces of carry-on luggage and two little kids crawling beneath their parent's outstretched legs. I knelt down next to Maddie and waved.

She didn't appear to be surprised. She frowned and pulled out her earbuds. I could hear the music, but I didn't recognize the tune.

"Hi, Dev."

"Hi, Maddie. Hey, I'm on your flight. I'm going to Paris."

"Yeah, so I heard."

"Umm, okay." Apparently, Tubby had told her we'd be traveling together. Screw him, I thought. "I mean, I feel so bad about having to work the night of your graduation, I canceled everything I had scheduled for the coming week and bought a ticket to Paris on the same flight as you."

"You bought the ticket?" she said, sounding like she didn't believe me.

"Yeah, you can ditch me if you want to, but I'd sure like to spend some time with you. Try and make it up to you."

"Make it up to me? God." She shook her head.

"Well, I can try. I know your graduation was a once in a lifetime event, and I couldn't make it. But a week in Paris. We can have a pretty good time."

She seemed to ignore my comment. She refocused on her cellphone and said, "Where are you sitting?"

I pulled out my boarding pass and doubled checked the seat assignment. "Steerage," I half-joked. "Fifty-one C. Where are you sitting?"

"Three B. Tub . . . I mean, my uncle booked me up in first class."

"Wow, pretty impressive. You'll arrive in Paris about four seconds before me."

"Yeah, I guess so."

She looked at me for a moment and shook her head. She put one of the earbuds back in her right ear. "Well, guess I'll see you in Paris," she said. She put the other earbud in her left ear and began typing a text message with her thumbs.

I'd been put down before, but this was major league. As far as she knew, I'd ponied up to pay for my flight. Paid a big chunk of change for the ticket, and she seemed bored by the whole idea. I sort of shrugged, stood up, and walked towards the boarding area. They hadn't called anyone to board and wouldn't for another thirty minutes or so, but already people were hovering near the entrance to the jetway. Based on Maddie's less than warm response, it wasn't going to be much of a problem to end things before they got started.

Thirty minutes later, they began the routine of calling people to board, folks needing help, people traveling with infants, and then first-class passengers. Maddie boarded with about twenty other people. She made a point of not acknowledging me as she walked by and handed her boarding pass to the woman scanning barcodes at the counter. Of course, I was seated in the zone furthest away from her. I waited on the jetway for another fifteen minutes taking baby steps toward the door to the plane. When I finally stepped on board, the flight attendant smiled, looked at my boarding pass, and pointed me down a long aisle. I looked over her shoulder into the first-class section. Everyone was seated in comfortable seats that stretched out into beds, and two flight attendants were busy serving chilled glasses of Champagne.

I recognized two guys seated in business class from high school. The Merda brothers. They were supposed to be twins, but they didn't look anything alike. Anthony, more commonly referred to as Big Tony, was a five foot three-inch fireplug. His supposed twin brother, Cyrus, was called Lurch because he was six feet plus a couple of inches. They were only in high school through the ninth grade. They served the next three years in the Red

Wing Juvenile Facility after being found guilty of breaking and entering, armed robbery, and assault. Pretty big charges for a couple of fourteen-year-olds. I'll give them this much. They learned their lesson. They were charged for a number of crimes over the years but never convicted again. I don't think they recognized me, and I certainly didn't acknowledge the two of them.

By the time I made it to my seat, all the overhead bins were full. Since I didn't have any luggage to store up there, it wasn't a problem. A girl about eighteen was sitting in my row. She glanced at me, and when I nodded, she quickly returned to looking out the window. I sat in the aisle seat and crossed my fingers that the space between us would remain empty.

I got my hopes up over the course of the next fifteen minutes. The seat between us appeared to be the only one that remained empty. No one had boarded the plane in the past five minutes. Just when I thought we were going to get some extra room, a very large man strolled onto the plane. He carried a small backpack, and the flight attendant at the door pointed him in our direction.

He was dressed in a pink golf shirt and one of the largest pairs of blue jeans I'd ever seen. I think he was wearing a belt, but his massive belly hung down over the waist on the jeans. He was large enough that he had to turn sideways to make his way down the aisle. He kept coming closer and closer, his belly jiggling with every step until he finally stopped next to me and said, "Pardonne moi monsieur, but I'm in your middle." He said in a heavy French accent. He proceeded to open all the overhead compartments looking for a place to store his backpack. He didn't find one.

I climbed out of my seat so he could squeeze into the middle. He smiled, leaned forward, and raised the seat arm between us. He wedged himself into the middle seat, oozed over half of my seat, and shoved his backpack beneath my seat. Once he was settled, he pressed the call button for a flight attendant.

He was oozing so far into my seat I had to push his fat away. His side flopped back on top of me and took up so much space that there wasn't room for my left arm.

"Yes sir," the flight attendant said as she reached over and turned off the call button. "What can I do for you?"

"The seat belt extension is needed," he said, holding up the end of his seat belt that clearly wouldn't fit around him.

"Maybe you could move me to another seat, and that would give this gentleman some more room," I pleaded.

"I'm sorry sir, but I'm afraid we have a completely full flight today. I'll be just a minute and back with the extension."

Eleven

I think we were somewhere over Ohio when the flight attendants started serving dinner. There was no way my fat seatmate was going to be able to lower his tray table. His huge belly nearly touched the seat in front of him, literally hanging just two or three inches from the seat. As we flew, I could feel his massive body jiggling against me.

"Dinner?" The flight attendant asked as she pushed her cart alongside me.

"What are the choices, monsieur?" Fatty asked.

"Today, we have chicken risotto and beef with broccoli."

"Oui," he said.

"Sir?"

"I shall have them both."

"I'm afraid I can only give you one," she said. She had a look on her face that was part disbelief and part 'Wait till I tell everyone about this.'

"Such a pity. I shall take the beef. If there is an extra chicken left, I will desire it."

"Sir?" She said and smiled at me.

"I'll have the chicken."

I pulled my tray table down or at least attempted to pull it down. It would only go down about two-thirds of the way before it rested at an angle on the guy's belly. She set my food tray down as if nothing was wrong. The tray slid forward and rested against the seat in front of me. The fat guy didn't even attempt to pull his tray table down. He simply held onto his meal, let it rest on his fat belly, and started shoveling in the food.

I waited another ten minutes before I looked behind me. The aisle was clear, and I folded my tray table up, grabbed my unopened food tray, and climbed out of my seat. Fatty acted like this was just an everyday occurrence, which, if he flew a lot of miles, it probably was. I walked back to the rear of the plane, set my food tray on the counter, opened it up, and started eating.

Halfway through my meal, a flight attendant came around the corner. He gave me a sort of surprised look and said, "Oh, I'm sorry, sir. This is a restricted area. I'm afraid I'm going to have to ask you to return to your seat."

"I don't have a seat."

"Sir?"

"Fifty-one C. Go check it out. You've got me next to one of the fattest people I've ever seen in my life. He's taken up half of my seat. He's so fat I can't even get my tray table all the way down."

"I'm sorry sir, but I'm afraid you'll—"

"It's okay, Mark. I'll take care of this." The flight attendant who had delivered my meal smiled at me. "How's the chicken?"

"Thanks. Chicken's okay. I'm sorry, but I didn't have any room up there. I'm afraid that fat guy has probably suffocated the poor girl next to the window."

"I think she's pretending to be asleep or praying that she will go to sleep. How about some wine?"

"Yeah, thanks, that would be nice."

She pulled a cart out from beneath the counter. "White?"

"Yeah, please."

She handed me a plastic glass and twisted the cap off the wine bottle, filled my glass almost to the top, and replaced the cap on the bottle. "Sorry about the seating. We have no control over that."

"You should make him pay for two seats," I said and stuffed the last piece of chicken into my mouth.

"Oh, if only we could. A lot of people think that's the answer. Of course, you can imagine the uproar if we asked passengers what their weight was when they purchased a ticket."

"Actually, after this experience, I'd be all for that."

"We don't see it too often, but it happens. Tell you what, why don't you take this seat, I can take one up in the next section." She pointed to one of two seats meant for flight attendants. "My name's Carol. I'll spread the word. But just in case someone gives you a hard time, tell them I said you should sit there."

"Oh, thank you. I don't know how I was going to survive. Can I ask you to do one more favor?"

"You can ask, but no promises."

"Could you tell that guy he can move into my seat. Maybe give that girl in the window seat some breathing room."

"I think I can do that. When you're finished with your dinner, pull the trash bin out." She pointed to a metal cabinet door. "You can lift that little lever on the back wheels with your foot, and it will roll out. I'll check back in a couple of minutes to make sure you did it properly."

She returned about five minutes later. I'd placed the plastic food tray in the trash bin, pushed the bin back in the cabinet, and locked the wheels.

"How'd I do?"

"Surprisingly well, you're hired."

"No thanks, I don't think I could be as polite and nice as you have to be."

She laughed at that. "Are you staying in Paris?"

"Yeah. It's kind of a long story, but I've never been before, and I want to check it out."

She handed me a business card. "Well, if you get bored, give me a call. I'm in Paris a few times every month. I wrote the hotel number on the back. I fly back to the states on Sunday."

"Thanks, Carol, and thank you for taking such good care of me."

"My pleasure, Mister Hassle."

"Please call me Dev," I said, not bothering to correct her.

Twelve

At some point, I must have dozed off because I snored myself awake. I had to have been out for at least a couple of hours. Carol and two other flight attendants were in the process of rolling breakfast carts out from beneath the counter. "We should be landing in about seventy-five minutes, Dev. How about some breakfast. We've got a cinnamon roll and some vanilla yogurt."

"I'll take it."

"Coffee?"

"Please, black."

She poured me a cup, handed it to me, and wheeled her cart up the aisle. She wasn't hard to look at. I watched as she headed back my way, one row at a time. She smiled at everyone as she passed out the breakfast meal and poured coffee. Eventually, she finished and rolled her cart back beneath the counter.

"How about another coffee?"

"I'd love it, thanks," I said and held out my cup.

She filled it, poured one for herself, and settled into the seat next to me. "Oh boy, long flight, but then, they're all long." She blew a gust upwards, fluttering her blonde bangs.

"I really can't thank you enough for letting me sit back here. I don't think I would have made it through the flight."

"Yeah, he's pretty big."

"Isn't there some way you could flag his name, put an emoji behind it so you'd know next time he books a flight he has to buy two seats."

"I wish we could. Ali Debauche is his name, by the way. French. We had a woman, oh maybe two years ago, who actually took up three seats."

"Three? What? Was she going to stretch out?"

"No. Unfortunately, she was that large. Sitting down, she covered all three of them. I've seen pictures of her somewhere on the internet. Thank God, the pictures weren't taken on one of my flights."

"Three seats? She must have weighed about four hundred pounds."

"We looked it up. She weighed six hundred and sixty-one pounds."

"Six hundred pounds?"

"Six hundred and sixty-one pounds."

"God. At what point do you start thinking maybe you should lose a couple of pounds? Was the plane even able to take off? Did it fly leaning to one side? Where do you even buy your underwear if you're that size?"

She laughed at that last question. "Oh, I don't know. I guess I never really thought about that. But you do have to wonder. Okay, I'd better get a move on and pick up the remnants of breakfast. We're going to be landing soon. I've enjoyed chatting with you, Dev."

"I've enjoyed it, too. Thanks for looking after me, Carol."

"Not a problem." She unbuckled her seat belt, pulled a grey trash cart out from the cabinet with a metal door, and headed back up the aisle.

As soon as the plane docked at the terminal and the fasten seat belt sign went off, I was out of my seat and hurried up the aisle. I made it past maybe a dozen rows before everyone was standing, pulling bags out of the overhead compartments and blocking the aisle from any further progress.

I stepped off the plane about twenty minutes later. We had a long walk to the French passport control area. I scanned my passport, got a sheet of paper with my passport information, a picture of me, and waited in line. I didn't see Maddie anywhere. After maybe fifteen minutes, I was waved up to the French officer sitting in a booth.

"Good morning," I said and handed him my passport.

He nodded and paged through the blank pages in my passport. He looked at me, looked at my photo, stamped my passport, and sent me on my way. I spotted a nervous looking Maddie in the baggage claim area waiting at carousel six. She caught sight of me and frantically waved me over.

"How'd it go flying first class, Maddie?"

She ignored my question. Silly me, she had no time for small talk. "The suitcase is green. It's large, and it's got a yellow ribbon around the handle."

"Yeah, my flight turned out to be pretty good. It started out with this big—"

"Hey, Dev. Green, really big with a yellow ribbon around the handle. Get it now and hurry up. We have to get to the bus that takes us into the city. It leaves from the next terminal in twenty-two minutes."

"Okay. You wait here, and I guess I'll get the luggage."

"Hurry."

The carousel was long with a ramp at the far end where luggage came down. As I hurried along looking for Maddie's suitcase, I couldn't help but feel I'd lost just about all desire to spend any time with her. I spotted a suitcase just ahead, large and green, but there was no yellow ribbon on the handle. Further up, I spotted another green suitcase and hurried to grab it. The thing was large. Larger than most of the other bags and heavy.

Along with the yellow ribbon around the handle, it had a red tag that read 'HEAVY.' The tag wasn't lying. I almost threw my back out, lifting it off the carousel. I figured Maddie must have packed every bit of clothing she owned. As I headed back to her, I spotted my suitcase, about one-third the size, and grabbed that as well. I placed it on top of Maddie's, took hold of the handle and wheeled them over to her.

"Okay good. Come on, we've got to make that bus," she said and hurried out the door. I guessed that was the signal that I was in charge of both suitcases. As I followed her, I glanced back and saw the fat guy Ali Debauche in the process of waddling into the baggage claim area.

Thirteen

Maddie seemed to know where she was going, and we arrived on the corner where we caught the bus to central Paris with fifteen minutes to spare. We waited outside another terminal with maybe a half dozen other people.

"Hey, Maddie. Can you keep an eye on the suitcases? I'm going to go inside and change some dollars into euros."

"I believe my uncle's instructions were that you are to stand guard over the luggage at all times unless it's in my hotel room."

"You kidding me? Come on. You can see the currency exchange booth through that window. See the white sign with the blue letters? I'm just going in there. I'll be back in a couple of minutes."

"So take the luggage with you."

"Really? You can't watch it?"

"That wouldn't be following Tub . . . err, my uncle's directions now, would it?"

"Okay, okay. We certainly wouldn't want to disobey your uncle. Here let me give you this cash, and you can go in and change this stuff into—"

"Are you listening? No. You want to do that? Go ahead and do it. Just take the suitcases with you. What's the big deal?"

I bit my tongue, took a deep breath, and hurried into the building. Fortunately, there was no one in line ahead of me. It took about three minutes. The woman told me what the exchange rate was and gave me a receipt. Not that it made any difference, I needed the cash. I hurried back out to Maddie. The bus arrived a few minutes later. The driver groaned, hoisted Maddie's suitcase into the luggage area underneath the bus, and gave me a dirty look. Once he was finished loading the luggage, he opened the door to the bus, and we began to board.

Most people had tickets. We didn't. As Maddie stepped onto the bus, she made sure she bounced going up the two steps. She flashed a sexy smile at the driver, pointed to me, and walked back to a seat. I paid eighteen euros apiece for two tickets, walked back to Maddie and sat down in the seat next to her.

"Dev, oh my God, don't touch me. You're all sweaty. Move over."

I moved in closer to her.

"Oh, God, gross. You are so gross. Move over the other way, you dope," she said and then hit me twice on the arm.

"You know, Maddie. I've had—"

"Please, don't talk to me. Just look out the window and practice your French or something."

An hour later, the bus pulled to a stop in a little square behind the Paris Opera House. There were six different streets leading into the area, and cars seemed to be going every which way. Everyone climbed off and waited while the suitcases were taken off. When it was time for Maddie's green suitcase to be pulled off, I said, "I got this."

The driver looked at me, stepped back, and in a heavy French accent said, "Help yourself."

I grunted a couple of times and finally got the thing onto the sidewalk. I placed my suitcase on top of Maddie's and looked around for our hotel. "You know which direction the hotel is?"

"Sort of," Maddie said.

We were standing in front of the Lindt Chocolate shop, and I figured this might be a good way for us to get back on track. "Hey, Maddie, it's the Lindt Chocolate shop. Want to check it out?"

She glanced at the shop, shook her head, and said, "No." She flashed a disgusted look in my direction and stuck her hand out to hail a cab.

A guy screeched to the curb thirty seconds later. I loaded the suitcases into the trunk and climbed into the taxi. Maddie handed the driver a card with the name and address of our hotel. He glanced at it, nodded, and pulled away from the curb. It was maybe a ten-minute drive back and forth on streets that all looked the same. I had a sneaking suspicion he was taking the long way, possibly driving back and forth on the same streets, but I couldn't prove it.

He suddenly screeched to a stop in front of the Paris Hotel. An attractive, four-story brick structure with a green awning in the middle of the block. Who would have thought Tubby booked us into a nice hotel?

Maddie hurried into the hotel while I paid for the taxi. The driver opened the trunk and pulled out my suitcase. He fumbled around, setting my suitcase on the sidewalk until I reached in and pulled out Maddie's monstrosity. I could hear my back as it made a snap, crackle, pop sound. The driver half laughed, slammed the trunk closed, hurried back behind the wheel and sped off. I wheeled the luggage into the lobby.

Fourteen

The guy behind the front desk was in the process of handing Maddie her room key. Actually, a plastic card that would unlock the door. "Oh, Dev, perfect timing. Come on. You can bring that up to my room. It's on the third floor."

"Sure thing," I said, thinking I couldn't wait to get rid of the suitcase and Maddie. "Just let me check into my room."

She cocked a hip, crossed her arms over her chest, and gave me a look.

At this point, I was so fed up with the attitude none of that worked. "Hi," I said to the guy behind the counter. "Do you speak English?"

"But of course, Monsieur."

"My name is Dev Haskell," I said and unzipped a pouch on the front of my suitcase. I pulled out my reservation and handed it to him.

He glanced at it, smiled, and began clicking keys on his computer. "Yes, here we are, room 210. I'll need your credit card, sir."

"A credit card? Isn't it already paid for?"

"No, sir, only reserved."

I looked at Maddie.

"Mine was paid for. Too bad. Guess he must like me better."

'Shit.' I pulled my wallet out and handed him my credit card.

"Thank you, sir."

A moment later, we were on the elevator heading up to the third floor. The elevator had just enough room for both of us with the luggage as long as I didn't breathe. Once we made it to the third floor, Maddie stepped off and headed down the hallway. I wrestled the luggage off the elevator and followed.

Her room turned out to be a suite that overlooked the street. It featured a small couch and two wing back chairs with a coffee table in the center. "You can put my luggage in the bedroom," she said.

I was only too glad to be rid of it. I wheeled the luggage into the bedroom and parked it next to the king-size bed. I pulled my suitcase off, and as I did, I noticed the black leather name tag hanging from the handle for the first time. Ali Debauche. It rang a bell, and then it dawned on me. The fat guy next to me on the plane.

"Hey, Maddie. Get the hell in here."

"Now, what is it?" She said, standing in the doorway.

"The name tag on this damn suitcase. It's not you. What the hell is going on here?"

"Yeah, so? It's, umm, probably my uncle's. So?"

"Your uncle? Really? What's his name?"

"I have more than one uncle," she said, suddenly sounding very nervous.

"Think you can you remember his name?"

"Don't be silly."

"Oh, believe me, I'm not being silly. What's the guy's name."

"Why are you asking me, it's right there on the suit-case and—"

"Suitcase? This thing's heavy as hell. What's going on here?"

"I already told you. It belongs to my uncle. He let me use it."

"Okay, what does he look like?"

"Look Like?"

"Yeah, describe him."

"Dev, You know who he is. Jesus, calm down and give it a rest. We both have been on a plane for about a hundred hours. Now, we're finally in our hotel. Hey, know what I think I might like to do right now?" She suddenly strutted toward me, undoing a button on her blouse with each step until she stood just an inch or two away from me. Only the bottom button on her blouse was still attached. "Want to get comfortable?" She said as she undid the last button and pushed out her bottom lip.

"Who in the hell is Ali Debauche?"

Fifteen

She wasn't making any sense. "Why in the hell would you take someone else's luggage? Especially something that heavy?"

"I already told you. Tub . . . err, my uncle wanted me to pick it up once I got to Paris."

"Okay, back the hell up, and you better start coming clean because I've had enough of your bullshit and the princess attitude."

"But I already told—"

"Will you please listen for a moment. So far, all you've done is lie to me."

She was sitting on the end of the king-size bed. Tears started to run down both her cheeks. As a final attempt to get me to dial down, she pulled her unbuttoned blouse off her shoulders and raised her eyebrows in a suggestive manner. "Interested?"

"Don't even think about it," I said, surprising even me. I think it was the first time in my life I'd turned down an offer. "First of all, Tubby isn't your uncle."

"Yes, he is. I swear he—"

"Maddie, I'm warning you. One more lie, and I'm calling the cops. I'm not kidding. Now you may not realize it, but there's an awfully good chance you've got us in some real trouble here. I'm going to ask you again, and I want a straight answer. How do you know Tubby Gustafson?"

"He's . . . He's my boss. He owns the club where I dance."

"The club where you dance. You're a stripper at the Centerfold Cabaret?"

"I prefer the term dancer, Dev, but yes. There, happy?"

"And Tubby's not your uncle?"

"I just told you that."

"Okay. So I'm guessing you didn't just graduate from law school."

"You kidding? I dropped out of high school in eleventh grade. So yeah, I'm all screwed up, and I'm stupid. There, satisfied?"

"Hey, calm down. I'm just trying to get some answers so we can figure out what we're going to do next."

"I thought you said you were going to call the cops."

"Only if you keep being a pain in the ass and lie to me. Look, however long you've known Tubby, I've—"

"Just since the first of the year. I started dancing at the Cabaret on New Year's day, and then last month, he asked me if I'd ever been to Europe."

"Have you?"

"You kidding? I've only been out of the state twice, and both times that was just to Wisconsin. I went to Hudson and worked a couple of stag parties on a boat on the St. Croix River. No, I've never been to Canada or Florida or California if that's what you're going to ask next."

"Okay, so tell me about the luggage."

"Tubby and that other guy that's always driving him around . . ."

"Fat Freddy Zimmerman?"

"Yeah, I think that's him. I mean, he's fat, so that's probably him."

"And he always drives Tubby around."

"Yeah, well, see they said they'd take me to the airport. And they gave me a suitcase just like that one. Only when I packed it, it didn't have any yellow ribbon on the handle. That was the night before I left and they said I had to pack my clothes in it. I didn't need anything that big. I just packed a dress, a couple pairs of shoes, jeans, some tops, and makeup and stuff. I even told them it was way too big. Then, Tubby, he gives me a thousand dollars, euros actually and he tells me because I've been such a good employee and all, I should go clothes shopping in Paris. Buy anything I want."

"When they took me to the airport, they helped me get my boarding pass and walked me to the security line. Tubby told me that Freddy guy, the driver, put a yellow ribbon on the handle of my suitcase, so in case there were others like it, I'd know which one was mine."

"So, you didn't put the ribbon on this handle?" I said and rolled the suitcase in front of her.

"No. I thought it was kind of strange. But then again, I've never traveled before, and Tubby was paying for it, and he gave me a thousand euros for clothes. I wasn't about to argue. Especially with Tubby."

"Didn't you think it was kind of strange, the thing was so heavy?"

"I never even lifted it, Fat Freddy did all that. They were so nice to me, and then the way you were, I maybe just thought you were being a pain in the butt. Besides, Tubby sort of warned me about you."

"Oh, great. And I suppose that night back in your apartment, the two of us. Tubby paid you to do that, too."

"Oh, no, that was real. Honest. But, he told me all about you being some sort of religious guy who was always trying to take the devil out of people. That's why he had me do the whole law school graduation thingy. So you wouldn't see me dancing. I know it sounds really dumb, but I thought he was trying to be nice to me. I never had a dad, and I kept thinking Tubby is what it would be like."

"Tubby? As a father? God."

"I didn't know."

"So, what happened to your suitcase?"

"You mean the one like this?" She nodded at the olive drab suitcase on wheels.

"Yeah, the one with all your clothes."

"I don't know. I thought it was kind of strange. Him putting the yellow ribbon on the handle. I mean, how many big green suitcases can there be?"

"Well, at least two that we know of."

"I'm trying to remember. But now that I look at it, it's sort of the same thing, only maybe a little different."

"Was your name on that other suitcase?"

"When he gave it to me, there was already a little tag with my name."

"And Tubby made the reservation in this hotel?"

"Yeah, and he paid for this room, too. Gave me a lot better deal than you got."

"Maddie, we're going to get out of here right now."

"Where do you want to go?" She said, sounding like I meant some designer clothing store.

"I mean, we're going to get out of this hotel. We passed another one, just two blocks away, but we have to get there and fast."

"Why?"

"Because whatever is in that thing. Someone is probably coming to get it. My guess is they're coming soon. So let's get out of here because they are not going to be very nice people."

"But I—"

"Maddie? Do you want to see Paris? Or better yet, do you want to make it home alive?"

"Well, yeah, of course."

"Okay, we need to leave. Now. Come on."

I tossed my suitcase on top of Maddie's and headed for the door.

"I can take yours," Maddie said. "I felt kind of bad, making you carry both of them."

Maybe there was hope. We took the elevator down to the main floor and wheeled our luggage across the lobby and out the door. We took a left and walked in the direction I thought I'd seen the other hotel. The street was narrow, and since there were cars parked halfway on the sidewalk as far as the eye could see, Maddie had to walk behind me. We were almost to the other hotel when a dark grey vehicle turned onto the street and raced up the slight hill. The car went right past us.

As the car approached, it appeared to lean decidedly to the right. When the car shot past, I saw two tough-looking characters in the front seat and caught the massive silhouette of none other than Ali Debauche in the back seat. Thankfully, the parked cars all along the street hid the olive drab suitcase I was pulling. The car ran through a red light and screeched to a stop two blocks behind us, in front of the hotel we'd just left.

I picked up my pace, and we hurried into the lobby of Hotel Joyce.

Sixteen

The Hotel Joyce was six-stories tall and located in the middle of the block. The front of the building was faced with a sort of buff-colored marble, and the upper floors were white with tall windows, faux balconies, and leafy green plants in front of each window.

The small lobby was empty, with the exception of a younger man in a suit coat seated behind the front desk. He stood as we entered, flashed a broad smile, and spoke in English. "How may I help you?"

"Hi. Hoping you might have a room available. I'm afraid we don't have a reservation."

"For how many nights, sir?"

I looked at Maddie and said, "Three nights?"

She nodded in agreement.

"Mmm, we do have a room. It's our suite, actually. If that would be acceptable?"

"Yes, that will do nicely."

"Very good, sir." He pushed a form and pen across the counter to me. "If you could just fill in some basic information, and I'll need a credit card if you'd be so kind."

I gave him my credit card and began to fill in my information. Amazingly, my card was approved, and in short order, we were headed towards the elevator. We took the elevator to the fifth floor.

"I've never been checked into two different hotels on the same morning," I said.

Maddie sort of gave me a look like it was an everyday occurrence. We stepped off the elevator and made our way down a winding hallway. She inserted the keycard in the lock. It clicked open and in we went. We entered a room with two couches facing one another in front of a white marble fireplace. A large antique gilt mirror hung over the fireplace. A small antique clock was centered on the mantel and ticking away.

"Oh, Dev, this is way better than the other place."

"Not to mention a lot safer."

A print of a Monet painting hung over a polished wood cabinet opposite the fireplace.

I placed Maddie's suitcase on its side or more accurately on its bottom and unzipped it. Crumpled, wrinkled clothes, huge shirts, gigantic boxers, extremely large trousers, along with awful smelly t-shirts and socks were all wrapped around a shiny metal briefcase. The briefcase was dimpled metal, worn, scraped, and scared in spots. It was about eight inches high and had two brass locks, one on either end.

I pulled open the three drawers in the cabinet beneath the painting. The first two were empty. The third held a half dozen round coasters for glasses and a wine bottle opener. I took the opener out of the drawer and pushed it closed. I placed the head of the wine bottle opener behind the portion of the lock meant to flip up and tried to force it. Nothing happened.

"Mind if I give it a shot," Maddie said.

"No offense, but if I'm not forcing it open, I doubt you—"

"Maybe just move aside, Dev, and let me give it a try."

As I moved over, she settled in front and leaned forward to examine the combinations on both locks. The dials on each one were set at 757. First, she tried 777 without any luck. She dialed in 555, and again, nothing happened. "Hey, wait a minute. God, if this works, it would be really bizarre," she said and dialed in 666 on the first lock and pushed the button. The lock snapped open. "Oh, my God. Can you believe it?"

"Try the other one, genius."

She dialed in 666 on the second lock, gave me a look, and pushed the button. The lock snapped open.

"Wait, don't open it up," I said.

"After all we've been through?"

"Move into the bedroom and let me open it."

"The bedroom?"

"In case they have some kind of device inside."

"Device?" She chuckled and shook her head.

"Yeah, you know, like a bomb or something."

"You think?" The smile suddenly disappeared as she rose to her feet and quickly backed up. "A bomb?"

"Probably not, but let's just play it safe."

"Mmm, yeah, okay," she said and hurried into the bedroom. A moment later, I heard the bathroom door in the bedroom close, and her muffled voice called "Okay, Dev. Go ahead."

I sat and stared at the metal briefcase in front of me, weighing the odds. Would it make sense to arm something if it held what? Gold bars. Silver ingots. Illegal drugs. No, it wouldn't. Especially, if it was going on an airplane for eight hours.

"Did you open it yet?" Maddie called.

"Still thinking about it. Give me another minute."

"Come on. I'm dying to see what's in there."

"Maybe think of a better choice of words."

"Oh, yeah. Sorry about that."

I took a deep breath and another one. Cautiously, I took hold of the briefcase and slowly lifted the top open. I sat there stunned and just stared.

After a minute or two, Maddie called, "Dev? Is everything all right?"

"Oh, yeah, Maddie. Sorry about that. It's okay. You can come out."

Seventeen

addie peeked into the room cautiously. I was still on my knees, staring into the open briefcase. "You sure it's okay?"

At the sound of her voice, I snapped back to reality and waved her in. As she approached, her eyes grew bigger, and she knelt down next to me. "Oh. My. God. Dev. Is that real?"

"It sure looks it."

The briefcase was filled with currency. From what I could see, hundred dollar bills were held together with mustard-colored bands. Each band had the figure **$10,000** printed across the front of the band. All the bundles were neatly stacked in the briefcase. I picked up a bundle and fanned it. All hundred dollar bills in the bundle with more layers below the one we were staring at.

"How much is in there?"

"A lot."

"What the hell was Tubby involved in?"

"He had us rip someone off," I said.

"What?"

"The name on the luggage tag. It says, Ali Debauche. That just happened to be the fat guy who sat next to me on the plane. He was so fat I had to get another seat. They put me in one of the flight attendant seats in the back of the plane. Just a coincidence that he was next to me, I think. Anyway, when we were walking to this hotel, a car raced past us, and he was sitting in the back seat."

"How do you know it was him?"

"Not that many people as fat as him, even in a city this size. They pulled to a stop in front of that other hotel. No wonder," I said and nodded at the currency.

"The other hotel? But how did they—"

"Did you have something in your suitcase that would identify you. A copy of your hotel reservation. Your flight reservation? Something that—"

"I had copies of both of those things."

"That's how they knew where to find you, and it means they know your name. And that's why Tubby had me come along. To get this out of the airport and make sure you made it to the hotel."

"But all this money, it doesn't make any sense. Why put a bunch of money in a suitcase and bring it on a plane?"

"Tubby probably paid Ali Debauche for something. Ali packs this cash in his suitcase. Tubby has access to the suitcase and puts the yellow ribbon on the handle after it's dropped off. Ali was waddling into the luggage area as we left. He got your hotel information going through your luggage. The suitcase looks the same as his. You said Tubby gave you the suitcase?"

"Yeah."

"I think it's probably a pretty safe bet that this Ali guy isn't too happy right about now."

"What are we going to do?"

"First of all, we're going to keep a very low profile. You have your cellphone?"

"Yeah," she said and pulled it out of the front pocket of her jeans.

"Turn it off."

"What?"

"Turn it off, Maddie. All this cash. They'll find a way to trace your cellphone, so they can find you. Find us. Turn it off now."

"But—"

"Maddie. Do you have any idea what they're going to do to us? They're not going to just nicely ask you for the money. We'll be able to identify them."

"But what if we tell them we won't—"

"Maddie. We're not dealing with nice people here. Tubby is not a nice person. He set you up. You were going to take the hit if the money was discovered. Although, why in the hell they'd ship all this cash instead of just doing a wire transfer doesn't seem to make any sense."

"Maybe it's stolen money. Somehow Tubby knew it was being transported, knew what kind of suitcase and he set the whole thing up. He told me about the yellow ribbon. How many green suitcases like this did you see at the airport on that baggage carousel?"

"Umm, there was one other one.

"That was probably mine, with all my clothes."

"And this one with the yellow ribbon on the handle. Tubby had access to it in the airport before the flight took off."

"What? He was with me the whole time. I would have seen him."

"Tubby and his connections. Somehow he and Fat Freddy got through security at the airport. They talked to me in one of the bars. They had TSA tags on their coats. They didn't just get past security. They were pretending to be security. Somehow they got this suitcase through security and onto the plane. All you, or we had to do, was pick it up and get it out of the terminal before that fat guy Ali Debauche could collect it."

"So, now what?"

"First things first, turn off your phone."

She frowned but pushed a button and held it down for a few seconds. The phone played a little tune as the screen went black. "Oh, God," she said and sounded worried.

I took my phone out and turned it off. "Okay, there, we're even. Hopefully, that will make it just that much harder for them to find us. I think it might be a good idea if we keep a low profile. Maybe plan on eating dinner in the room tonight and not going out while we figure how to get out of this mess."

"A low profile? Dev? We're in Paris."

"Yeah. And right now I'm thinking there are some pretty pissed off guys looking for us. I don't know about you, but I'd like to stay alive."

"What are we going to do?"

We heard a siren in the distance, gradually growing closer. Pim-pon, pim-pon, pim-pon. We both hurried to the window and peeked out. A Paris Police car raced past the hotel. The car was a white compact with red stripes along the side and the word POLICE in blue letters on the door. Just as the sound began to fade, it stopped altogether.

"Oh-oh."

"What?" Maddie said attempting to lean out the window.

"I think the car stopped. Maybe just a block or two away. It might be at the other hotel."

"The one we just left?"

"Could be."

Maddie tried to angle her head out the window for a better view. It didn't work.

"All right, let's calm down for a minute. We need to think of some options." Maddie stepped back from the window and took a seat on one of the couches. I pulled the window closed and sat down opposite her. Occasionally we glanced over at the open briefcase full of cash.

"I suppose we could count it," she said.

Eighteen

We heard two more sirens racing past on the street below while we counted the cash. We fanned each bundle the first time through. Just like the first one I checked, they were all hundred dollar bills. We counted the money a total of four times. We counted it together twice. Maddie counted it again because she couldn't believe it. Once she was finished, I counted it again because I still couldn't believe it. One hundred bundles. Ten grand a bundle. One million dollars. It was fair to say neither one of us had ever seen that much cash before and probably never would again if we lived that long.

"Oh. My. God." Maddie said, not for the first time.

"Oh, we are so screwed."

"Screwed? Dev, what are you talking about? We'll never, ever have to work again. I can stop dancing and buy a fancy house and a Volkswagen Beetle."

"What?"

"Yeah, a Volkswagen Beetle, a convertible. A red one."

"Maddie. Just in case you forgot, let me remind you. This money isn't ours. It's not yours, and it's not mine.

The guy whose suitcase this was in, that Ali Debauche guy. He's probably rather upset because we have all his money right now. He had two thugs with him in the car that drove past. I would guess, right about now, he's calling everyone he knows and telling them to be on the lookout for you. He'll be offering a very nice reward to whoever finds you. Oh, and one other problem. Because Tubby told you to grab the suitcase with the yellow ribbon. And Tubby was most likely the guy to put the yellow ribbon on that handle, to begin with. I'd say it's a pretty safe bet Tubby is sending someone to take this money from you. Most likely a number of someones. They were probably on the same flight as us and may not be too interested in being nice."

"But why would—"

"Maddie, hello? You were set up. We both were. I can see the headline. Two American tourists end up in a bad part of Paris."

"But I bring a lot of business into the Centerfold Cabaret for him. Give me one good reason why he would do this."

"One good reason? I can give you a million good reasons."

"Oh, yeah. So, what do we do now?"

"First of all, we have to get out of town. I know it's a big city, but the odds of someone seeing us are increasing by the hour. We can rent a car, drive somewhere, and fly out of a different airport. Maybe even a different country. We keep a low profile. No offense, but you need to change your hair color.”

“What? Dev, this is how I make my living. You know how many guys ask the bartenders when the fox with the yellow hair is on stage?”

“Yeah, and anyone looking for you will be able to spot you a mile away. How many women in this town have their hair colored like that? Don’t bother to answer. I’ll save you the time. Zero. So part of keeping a low profile is to make sure we’re not standing out in a crowd. Make sense?”

“Yeah, maybe.”

“Okay, good. We’ll take care of that tomorrow. For right now, we just better hang tight. I don’t know about you, but the time change is starting to catch up to me. Let’s hit the sack, sleep, and then we’ll figure out what we’re going to do about dinner.”

“How about a little something for lunch?”

“You mean go out to lunch?”

“Relax, Mister Tight Control. There was a buffet area downstairs, just past the front desk where we checked in. I need a little roll or something, maybe a yogurt if they have any. But not raspberry. Just vanilla or banana if they have it.”

“Vanilla or banana?”

“Yeah, or strawberry. Just don’t bring back any raspberry. I don’t like all the seeds in raspberry. It gets so gross. It makes me—”

"I get it. No raspberry. Okay. Done. I'll go down and try and get you something. Anyone knocks on the door. You don't let them in unless it's me. Got it?"

She gave me a bogus salute using her left hand.

"I'm serious, Maddie. No one in unless it's me."

Nineteen

I pulled the door to the room closed behind me and waited until I heard her click the locks. To double-check and make sure it was locked, I tried the doorknob before I headed down the hall. I pushed the button for the elevator and waited for an interminable amount of time. It was probably only about thirty seconds. Although, it felt like an hour. Finally, I headed down the staircase and stepped out on the ground floor as three people and four suitcases attempted to squeeze onto the elevator.

Curiosity got the best of me, and I walked across the lobby and stepped out of the front door just long enough to glance up the street. The police car we'd heard out the hotel window appeared to be parked in front of our former hotel. Only now it was joined by two other police cars and an ambulance with its rear doors open. The entrance to that portion of the street was now blocked off. Two uniformed officers stood in the middle of the street, denying access to any and all vehicles.

I stood and stared for three or four minutes. As I was about to step back into Hotel Joyce, two uniformed men wheeled out a hospital gurney with what looked like a body bag on top of it. A large medical kit rested on top of the body bag, and the guys pushing the gurney didn't seem to be in any sort of hurry. That was more than enough for me to see, and I hurried back into our hotel.

I crossed the lobby and went into a room that had apparently been a courtyard at one time. Now it was a dining area with a glass-roofed ceiling and soft music playing in the background. At the far end of the room were three large platters with a variety of different breads and rolls piled on top. I took two small plates, placed four croissants on the plates along with little containers of butter, honey, and strawberry jam. I hurried onto the elevator and back up to our room on the fifth floor. I ran down the hall and knocked on our door.

"Who is it?" Maddie called out a moment later.

"It's me, open up."

"Dev?"

"Yeah, Maddie, open the door."

The door opened a crack. The latch was still in place as Maddie peeked out to make sure it was me. She closed the door. I heard the latch unlock, and she opened the door wide enough to let me in. As soon as I hurried inside, she closed the door behind me.

"What's with you?" she said as I unloaded the plates on the cabinet beneath the Monet print.

"I took a moment to look out on the street toward our first hotel."

"And?"

"The street is blocked off by police cars. There are two cops directing traffic, not letting anyone drive past the hotel. Then just as I was about to go back inside, two guys wheeled out a gurney with a body bag."

"A body bag? Are you sure?"

"Take my word for it. I've seen enough of them. It was a body bag. And yes, before you ask. There was a body in it."

"But who could it be?"

"I'd say the odds are pretty good it wasn't some senior citizen who'd had a heart attack. Remember, I said that car raced past us with the fat guy when we were walking down here?"

"Yeah. You said he's Ali something."

"Ali Debauche is his name. My guess, the front desk guy wouldn't give them your room number. Maybe told them he was going to call the cops or something and they killed him. Probably got the room number and kicked the door in. It's just a good thing we weren't in there. They couldn't have missed us by more than five minutes."

"Maybe we should get out of here now."

"This might be the safest place to be. The room's in my name, so even if the bad guys check here, there's no listing of you. Whoever Tubby sent is probably scratching their head right now and not sure what to do. I think the best thing for us is to eat these croissants and try and get some sleep. I'm thinking we get out of town first thing in the morning. Right after you get a new hair color."

We devoured the croissants. I stared at the last one after already eating two.

"If you want, we could split it," Maddie said.

"No, thanks, but you go ahead. I've already had two."

She didn't have to be told twice. She snatched the croissant off the plate. Slapped some butter on the end, drizzled honey over it, and took a large bite. She wolfed the thing down in three bites and burped after her final swallow.

"Oh, sorry. God, what a piggy. But I was so hungry, and they were so good."

I got up, unlocked the door, and hung the 'Do Not Disturb' sign out in the hall. After locking the door, I grabbed a wooden chair from next to the cabinet and wedged that beneath the doorknob.

"If you don't mind, I'm going to grab a quick shower before I hit the sack," I said.

"Not a problem. In fact, I'll take one after you."

"You want to go first?"

"No thanks. You go ahead."

I took my time in the shower. I stood under the hot water and let it run over me while I tried to figure out what in the hell we were going to do. I finished the shower without coming up with any answers. I dried off, stepped out of the bathroom and into the bedroom. The white duvet was pulled back on the bed. Maddie was stretched out on the bed in a white terrycloth robe with the hotel logo embroidered on the right breast. As I stepped toward the bed, she raised up on one arm and gave me a sexy smile.

"Your turn," I said, indicating the bathroom.

"I was thinking, I might give it a miss for a little minute."

"What?"

She sort of rolled her eyes and pulled the robe back, exposing her thigh up to about her hipbone. She raised her eyebrows and said, "Hello."

"Oh, yeah. Sure thing. I'm all for it. Might as well enjoy the moment." I dropped the towel on the floor and slid onto the bed. It was bumpy and uncomfortable. And I moved back and forth, trying to find a comfortable spot, all the while failing miserably.

"What the hell is with this bed? It—"

"Dev. You ever sleep on a million dollars before?"

"What?" I half laughed. "No. I never . . . Oh, don't tell me. Is that what I'm lying on? All those bundles of cash?"

"Just once, let's sleep on them. And, before we go to sleep . . ."

"You mean do it on a million dollars?"

"Well, have you ever?"

"Actually, no. Come to think of it, that sounds like a really cool idea."

Fifteen minutes later, Maddie tossed her robe over a chair and strutted into the bathroom. I wiggled around for a minute or two, trying to get comfortable. Nothing seemed to work, and I finally gave up and just fell asleep.

When I woke, Maddie was snuggled against me, sound asleep, and breathing deeply.

Twenty

I quietly pulled a terrycloth robe from the Armoire on the far wall and tiptoed into the main room. I thought about looking out the window to see if the police cars were still up the street but just as quickly decided against it. It was dusk, and I guessed the time to be around seven or eight at night. I sat on the couch and thought about what our next move should be.

Maddie stepped out of the bedroom a half-hour later. I still hadn't come up with a plan. She pulled her robe closed and tightly tied the belt, eliminating any thoughts of a repeat match. "Have you been up long?"

"Not really. Maybe just thirty minutes. How'd you sleep?"

"Like the dead. Although it wasn't all that comfortable. My back is killing me." She moved her shoulders from left to right, then arched her back in an attempt to stretch it.

"Maybe sleeping on a million dollars isn't all it's cracked up to be."

"Yeah. Yet another disappointment in life. Hey, I'm going to hop in the shower. I'm so hungry I could eat a horse. Where do you want to go for dinner?"

"Right here. Let me call down to the front desk and see what's on the room service menu."

"No burgers. I want a real meal. No potatoes. A salad and vegetables would be nice and some sort of entree. Not fish. Well, unless it's fresh salmon. Oh, and some sort of hors d'oeuvres would be kind of nice."

"And dessert," I added.

"Oh, yeah. Mmm, I think—"

"Maddie, I was kidding. Look, I'm going to try and find a McDonald's or something."

"If you go out and get McDonald's, don't bother coming back. I think I earned a decent meal after my workout before our nap. I did not come to Paris to eat a cheeseburger."

"Are you forgetting what the hell happened today?"

"No. But that doesn't mean we have to be miserable. And while we're on the subject. I don't have anything to wear other than the clothes on my back. We will be taking care of that tomorrow before we go anywhere."

"Now, hold on just a minute. We—"

"No. You hold on, Dev. I already said I'd change my hair color. So why don't you just back the hell off? And if someone is going to kill me, I refuse to be found dead in clothes I've worn for three days straight. So, no. Don't argue. Just get dressed and come back with a decent meal."

I was about to say something, but she shoved her hand up in front of my face. "No. Not another word. I'm going to take a shower and get cleaned up while you make yourself useful and get dinner. Period. Not another word."

"Maddie, we have to—"

"Don't. Just don't." With that, she headed into the bathroom and slammed the door.

I got dressed, and once I heard the shower running, I went through her purse and found the envelope from Tubby with ten hundred euro bills. I grabbed two and went out to find a meal.

There was a little restaurant, just two doors down from the hotel. I walked in. The waitress smiled and said, "Good evening. Table for one?"

I wanted to ask her how she knew I couldn't speak French. Instead, I said, "Can I get a couple of meals to go and an hors d'oeuvre?"

"But of course, depending on what you order, it may be twenty minutes or so. You can stay and have a glass of wine while you wait."

That sounded like a pretty good idea. She handed me a menu with English translations. I ordered two meals, a cheese plate, two Crème brûlée for dessert, and a bottle of wine. I drank a glass of wine while I waited.

Maddie was still in the bathroom when I returned. I placed the shopping bag with our dinners on the floor in front of the fireplace. I opened the bottle of wine, settled onto one of the couches, and waited. Maddie eventually stepped out of the bathroom. She'd been in there for close to an hour. Not that I was going to mention it.

"Did you get dinner?"

"Yeah. I remembered you said you didn't want a cheeseburger. So, I got you a regular hamburger with—"

"Were you listening? I told you I—"

"Hey, relax, Crabby. I got two very nice dinners in the little restaurant a couple doors down. I got nice hors d'oeuvres, a bottle of wine. As long as we're stuck in this room, we may as well relax and enjoy ourselves."

"Really? You did that?"

"Yeah. Nothing's too good for you, Maddie."

"Mmm, I've heard that before. Can we eat? God, I'm absolutely starving."

"Yeah, tell you what. I'll set the table and dish us up, and you pour the wine."

I pulled the Styrofoam trays out of the bag and set them on the coffee table. I placed the tray with the cheese plate in the center and opened the tin foil around the sliced baguette. I folded the paper napkins in a triangle and set the plastic silverware on top of the napkins. Maddie brought over two plastic glasses from the bathroom and proceeded to fill them with red wine.

"Oh, the cheese looks delicious. What did you get for our main course?"

"Squid."

"What?" She stopped in midstream as she was about to open her Styrofoam tray. "Dev, I told you."

"Where's your sense of humor. It's some beef thing. The name was long and in French. So, I can't remember, but I think you'll like it."

She opened her tray and sniffed cautiously. A smile appeared on her face. "Oh, it smells delicious. Thank you. This is just what the doctor ordered." She took a large forkful of food, chewed once or twice, and said, "Mmm, so good. Thank you. It's so sweet of you to buy dinner."

"Actually, you bought dinner. Or, maybe more accurately, Tubby bought it. I took two hundred euros out of the envelope Tubby gave you."

"What?" She said and began to increase her volume with each successive statement. "You stole my money. You can't do that. That's my money. Tubby gave it to me to spend. Not you. Who do you—"

"Maddie, Maddie, Maddie. Calm down. We're sitting on a million dollars in cash here. We're not going to run out of money anytime soon. We'll change some bills into euros tomorrow and get you paid back. So relax."

Thankfully, she did calm down, and we spent a good hour leisurely eating our meal. We finished up with the Creme Brûlée. Maddie drank the last of the wine. We forced ourselves to stay awake until eleven, watching some show in French with bad guys robbing a bank.

I pulled the bundles of cash out from beneath the sheets on the bed and repacked them in the metal briefcase while Maddie snuggled into two or three pillows. We both fell asleep about thirty seconds after our heads hit the pillow.

Twenty-one

I woke well before Maddie. I got dressed and hurried down to the ground floor and the brunch room with the croissants. I loaded up a plate, poured two cups of coffee, placed lids on the paper cups, and took the elevator back to our room. Maddie was still asleep when I returned. I sat on the couch, eating my croissants, sipping my coffee, and enjoying the peace and quiet.

She woke a couple of hours later and made her way into the room. She looked only half awake. "Oh, boy. I must have really needed that. I don't think I even rolled over last night. What time is it?"

I glanced at the TV screen. I had a news station on with the sound off and a nonstop trail of headlines running across the bottom of the screen. Since it was all in French, I had no idea what the headlines said. The time was displayed in the corner. "It's seven twenty-one."

"In the morning?"

"Yeah."

"But I was so tired. How come I'm awake so early?"

"Jet lag. Your internal clock is all screwed up. Your head is still on Minnesota time. Central Standard. Paris time is seven hours ahead. You went to sleep at eleven.

That's ffour in the evening in your head, and you slept until one in the morning, Minnesota time. It takes a few days to get over it."

"Oh, God. No wonder I'm tired. I'd still be dancing for another hour if we were back home."

"I suppose that's one way to look at it."

She sat down on the couch across from me, oblivious to her robe hanging open. I certainly wasn't going to say anything.

"I got you some coffee and rolls. After you eat, let's get dressed and find a place to change some dollars into euros."

"I thought you did that at the airport," she said and followed up with a heavy dose of coffee.

"Yeah, I did, but I don't want us to use our credit cards. Just in case the people we're trying to avoid have some way to trace our cards."

"You think they could do that?"

"Why take the chance? We're sitting on all that cash. If we take a couple of bucks, I don't think anyone is going to miss it. Let's both take a grand. That's not out of line with what tourists would bring in to change. We'll take the bills from different bundles. I don't think that stuff is counterfeit, but it never hurts to play it safe. Then, once we get the cash exchanged, you can get your hair done, and we can get you some new clothes."

"We passed a bunch of shops when we got off the bus from the airport. If we can get back there, I can start shopping." The idea of clothes shopping in Paris seemed to wake Maddie up. She suddenly wolfed down another croissant and finished her coffee.

"Any more coffee?"

"I'll go down and get us two more. Why don't you start getting dressed? I'll ask for directions at the front desk for the closest currency exchange place."

"I'd take one sugar in my coffee and another croissant," she said and headed into the bedroom.

I left with my marching orders. It turned out there was a currency exchange office just three blocks away and a bank a block or two beyond that. I grabbed two more coffees, one with sugar, two more croissants, and headed back to the room.

Maddie was still in her bathrobe. She was back on the couch, flipping through channels on the TV when I came back into the room.

"What's the point of watching TV if I can't understand what they're saying?"

I set her coffee and croissants down in front of her. "I know it sounds strange, but since we're in France, almost everything is going to be in French."

She picked up her coffee and took a sip. "I thought I told you to put sugar in mine."

I made a face and swallowed the sip I'd just taken. "Sorry about that. I gave you the wrong one." We exchanged cups. "While you're drinking your coffee, maybe you should think about getting dressed, and we can exchange a little of that currency."

"I've been thinking about that, and I can see a problem."

"What kind of problem?"

"Are you planning to carry that metal briefcase with us?"

"No. It would be one more thing that would identify us. I have no doubt there are a lot of people on the street looking for us right now."

"Exactly. So if we both go to exchange currency, what do we do with the briefcase? Hide it under the bed?"

"I guess I hadn't thought about that," I said.

"Yeah, I figured as much. Here's my plan. We don't walk around town with all that money. I'll just stay here with the briefcase. You go exchange some bills. You come back with the euros. I get my hair colored and go shopping for some new clothes, and when I come back, we figure out a place to go."

I thought about that for a long moment, and the more I thought about it, the more sense it seemed to make. "Yeah, Maddie. A much better idea. Keep the 'Do Not Disturb' sign on the door. They gotta be used to people sleeping all hours of the day. Hopefully, they'll leave you alone. Let me grab some cash, and with any luck, I should be back in about thirty minutes."

I went into the bedroom and pulled the metal case out from underneath the bed. Maddie stood behind me as I pulled twenty bills from twenty different bundles. Two grand total. I placed the cash in my front pocket and grabbed my wallet and my passport.

"I'm just gonna grab a shower. So take your time," Maddie said.

It was the way she said it that gave me pause. "Yeah, let me just grab one more thing," I said and pulled her jeans off the stuffed chair next to the bed.

"What are you doing?"

"I'm taking your jeans. Just in case you were thinking about leaving while I was gone."

"You big creep. You really think I would do something like that?"

"Umm, yeah. I do. By the way, I'm going to tell the front desk that you're having an episode, and if they see you, they should call security and lock you back in this suite."

"You can't . . . that's crazy."

"No crazier than you thinking you'll just run off with this cash. Please don't. I'm taking these jeans for your own good, Maddie. You get spotted, for this amount of money, they'll kill you without a second thought." I rolled her jeans into a tight little bundle. Placed them under my arm and headed out the door.

"Dev. Dev, come on. Dev. Dev?"

Twenty-two

As I hurried down the street, I was convinced I'd just thwarted Maddie's plan of walking out the door with a million bucks. The directions to the Currency Exchange Office were to take a left at the corner and head down the street for three blocks. I could see the white sign with blue lettering over the Currency Exchange front door from two blocks away.

I walked past the place and went around the block and did the same thing again. Both times I peered in through the window to see if I might spot any questionable looking characters. The first time there was just a young couple at the counter, and the second time no one was in there. After my third trip around the block, I stepped inside. The office wasn't much wider than a hallway with a marble-topped counter and a woman seated behind thick panes of glass.

"Bonjour," she said as I approached the counter.

I smiled and said, "Parlez-vous, American?" Using what I thought was a French accent.

She seemed to cringe at my attempt and said, "Yes, certainly. You wish to obtain euros?"

"Yes," I said and took the wad of cash from my front pocket. I kept it hidden below the counter and quickly counted out ten hundred dollar bills. I placed the cash in the small pass-through well in the middle of the counter. She smiled, took the money, then reached for a marker, and ran it across the serial number on each bill. She placed the cash in a drawer, punched in a quick set of numbers on a keyboard, and began to count out a stack of fifty euro notes. She followed up with a twenty, a five, and some coins then added a receipt to the stack. She pushed the euros beneath the glass, smiled, and said, "Thank you."

I smiled back, stuffed the cash in my pocket, and headed out the door. I walked two blocks further on and spotted the bank. I went in and essentially went through the same process again, exchanging the last of my hundred dollar bills for euros. Upon leaving, I walked around the corner and headed in the opposite direction so I wouldn't repeat the same route in reverse. I got lost for about fifteen minutes, due to streets at different angles and all the buildings beginning to look the same. I finally made my way back to our hotel and hurried up to our room. The closer I got to the room, the more nervous I became.

What if Maddie had bought a pair of jeans off another guest or just walked out with the cash in her bathrobe? Why didn't I tell the clerk at the front desk that she was having some sort of episode and not to let her leave the hotel? What if that fat guy or whoever Tubby had sent found our new hotel?

"Maddie?" I half-shouted as I hurried into the room.

She wasn't sitting on one of the couches in front of the fireplace, and she wasn't looking out the window. I hurried into the bedroom. She wasn't in there either.

"Maddie, damn it."

"I said I'm in the bathroom. God, give me a minute, will you?"

"Oh, ahh, sorry. I wasn't sure you heard me."

"You kidding? Everyone in the entire hotel has probably heard you by now. Calm down, Mister Whacko. I'll be out in a minute."

"Not a problem. No rush." I tossed her jeans over the stuffed chair and hurried over to the bed. I pulled the metal case out from underneath and opened it up. If she'd taken any of the cash, I couldn't tell. Everything looked fine. A moment later, I heard the toilet flush. I closed the case, shoved it under the bed, and hurried back into the living room.

Maddie stepped out of the bathroom after a minute or two.

"Hey, I left your jeans on the chair in there. Nice day outside. Sunny. Warm." I didn't hear a reply and hurried into the bedroom. Maddie was lying on her back on the bed. Pulling her jeans on. "That's how you put those things on?"

"You weren't complaining when I was wearing them."

"No, I mean, they look great."

"So," she tugged the jeans up her thighs, raised her midsection off the bed, and pulled the jeans up over her thong. "Whew. Okay," she said, standing. She buttoned the jeans and zipped them. "I'm going to go get this hair dealt with."

"Ask at the front desk, and they can probably name a half dozen places to go. I'll stay here and watch the money."

"Sure you will. Just give me your jeans, and I'll get out of here."

"My jeans? You gotta be kidding me?"

"Hey, you didn't hear me complain when you took mine."

"Yes, I did. As a matter of fact, you called me a creep. Said I was crazy."

"And you've done nothing to change my mind. Now, hand them over. Come on. Off with them."

I gave her a disgusted look, then sat on the edge of the bed and pulled my jeans off. I pulled the euros out of my front pocket, counted off a thousand euros, and handed them to her. "This is for the hair, and you might as well get some clothes while you're at it."

"Thanks, I'll see you later."

"Hey, Maddie. Get the hair done first. They're going to be looking for someone with your current style, and it's unique. Very unique."

"That's exactly what I intend to do, and thanks. Okay," she said. She tossed my wallet and passport onto the bed. Rolled my jeans up, tucked them under her arm, and headed out the door. I hurried over to the window and looked out onto the street waiting for her to appear. I watched from five floors up as she stepped out of the hotel. She walked about five feet and hailed a cab. Good. At least she wouldn't be turning all sorts of French heads walking along the street with her yellow and green hair.

Twenty-three

It was a long afternoon. A very long afternoon. At ten o'clock, I was beginning to get nervous. How long does it take to buy a pair of jeans? By three o'clock, I was pacing. At four o'clock, I was planning various ways to kill her. At five o'clock, I pulled on a pair of shorts from my suitcase, dragged the metal briefcase out from beneath the bed, and headed for the door. I pulled the door open just as Maddie was about to insert her keycard in the lock.

"Dev?"

"Maddie?" I said, not quite recognizing her.

"Just where do you think you're going, Mister? And where did you get those shorts? They look dreadful."

I stepped back so she could enter the room. Her hair was short, maybe three inches long and brown. She looked about ten years younger, and I'm not a fan of short hair on women. She was carrying at least a half dozen different colored shopping bags in her hands. Each bag had some extravagant sort of logo and the fancy name of a store.

"Thinking of going somewhere with the cash?" She said, then kicked the metal briefcase, so it banged against my shin.

"Ouch. Hey, calm the hell down. No, I wasn't planning to go somewhere. Call me stupid, but since you took all day to find a pair of jeans, I was starting to worry about you. I thought I'd go look for you. Make sure you were okay."

"Thought you'd look for me? In Paris? And just where were you planning on looking?"

"All those fancy clothes shops," I said, nodding at the shopping bags. "And by the way. Your hair looks lovely."

She stared at me for a moment, not sure she should believe me.

"I'm serious, Maddie, it looks great. They did a really great job."

"Thanks. Here. Wait till you see what I got." She scattered the bags across one of the couches. They took up all the room. "Notice the jeans," she said, stepping back and sort of moving her legs back and forth before turning to the side and repeating the process. "Armani, I got 'em on sale for five hundred."

"Five hundred bucks for a pair of jeans?"

"No, five hundred euros, Dopey. Remember, we're in Paris."

"Oh, well, then. I suppose it's okay."

She ignored my comment and said, "Check this out. You like?" She pulled a red silk top out of a bag and held it up in front of her.

"Yeah, nice, very nice." What did I know?

She reached into a pink bag with a black bow at the top. The words Agent Provocateur were written in black script beneath the bow. "I got fitted for bras and strappies. You can't get this kind of quality back home." She pulled out a half dozen bras and various pairs of lacy underwear.

"Mmm-mmm, yeah, nice."

"Oh God. Why do I even bother."

"What do you have in the other bags?"

"Creams, makeup, hair conditioner, pretty much just the basics. Blouses, two sweaters, I got a windbreaker in case it gets windy, a few other things. Just the essentials, really. Right now, I need a shower. While I'm doing that, you can decide on where you plan on taking me for dinner?"

"I thought we'd do a repeat of last night. Grab a takeout and eat it up here in the room."

"No. Sorry. Not going to work. Dev, you barely recognized me when I was at the door. Whoever is looking for me is scanning the city for someone with yellow hair and green ends. They won't be looking for the new me."

"Okay, grab a shower and let me think about where we'll go."

"Fair enough. Just give me a couple of minutes, and we can still get in and beat the dinner crowd. I'm starving."

"Okay. Okay. Get going."

Maddie gathered up her bags and hurried into the bedroom. She closed the bathroom door behind her, and a few minutes later, I heard the shower running. I waited a few minutes until I was sure she was in the shower, then hurried into the bedroom and grabbed the cellphone out of my suitcase.

I pulled the check from Matteo Martin out of my wallet and dialed the number. The call didn't go through, and a moment later, a recording came on. Unfortunately, it was in French, and I had no idea what was being said. I turned my cellphone off and picked up the room phone.

"Front desk," a male voice answered.

"Yeah, I'm trying to make a call to the United States, but I get a recording, and I don't speak French. I was calling on my cellphone."

"You would have to dial zero to place an international call. Then, input the country code, which is the number one for the US. Then your code for the area and the phone number." I repeated the instructions. "Yes, that is correct."

"Thank you," I said and hung up. I followed his directions and finally input Matt's number. The phone rang a half dozen times before he answered.

"Yeah, this is Matt."

"Hey, Matt. Dev Haskell."

"That check should be good, Dev. Is there a problem?"

"No, no nothing like that. Here's the deal. I'm actually over in Paris at the moment and—"

"You're shitting me."

"No. Umm, we seem to have run into a bit of a problem. I'm thinking it might be a good idea if we maybe got out of town for a couple of days. Wondering if you got any ideas where we might go?"

"What kind of a problem. I got an uncle, retired now, but he used to be with the Police Nationale. If you're in some kind of trouble, he might be a good place to start."

"I don't think I'll need that, but maybe give me his name anyway. I was just looking for some sort of general tourist places. You know, out of the big city."

"Okay, you're sure you don't need help?"

"Yeah, pretty sure. I think."

"Okay, anything changes you get back in touch with me. My uncle is retired, but everyone on the force knows him, Henri Martin. I'll text you his phone number. I got a cousin who owns a bar up in the ninth arrondissement. The name of his place is Le Mondain." He spelled it out for me, and I wrote it down. "Nice joint. He's there every night, nice guy. Just ask for Jerome. He can tell you some out of the way places to visit. I'm guessing you maybe want to lay low?"

"Exactly."

"Yeah, he'll be able to give you some ideas."

"And his place is on Ninth Street?"

Matt gave half a laugh. "No, it's in the ninth arrondissement. Paris is divided into twenty sections called arrondissements, Dev. The ninth is in the center of the city. Any taxi guy will know where it is. You staying in a hotel?"

"Yeah."

"Have them look up the address for you and then grab a taxi there. You sure you're okay?"

"Yeah. Just need to cool our heels for a bit." I heard the shower turn off in the bathroom. "Thanks for your help, Matt. I better get going here."

"Any problems give me a call, Dev. Hope you're able to enjoy your time. It's a great place."

"Yeah, we'll be fine. Talk to you later, Matt. Thanks. Bye," I said and hung up.

"Who were you talking to?" Maddie said as she stepped out of the bathroom.

"Oh, just called the front desk to get a restaurant recommendation. They said the place I got the takeout last night is extremely good."

She looked like she didn't believe me.

"No, really, they did. And they gave me the name of a great place to get a glass of wine afterward. It's in the ninth arrondissement."

"What's that? A mall or something?"

"Oh, sorry, I thought you'd know. It's a section of Paris. There's twenty of 'em, sections."

"Hmm, yeah, whatever. Give me a couple of minutes to get ready, and we'll go."

Twenty-four

The "couple of minutes" turned into a lot longer. While I waited, I hid the bundles of cash beneath the cushions of the two couches then sat on one of the couches flipping through TV channels with the remote. Everything was in French. I ended up on a cartoon channel, and sort of got what was happening. Some dog, a French poodle, kept getting tricked by a cat. Just as Maddie came out of the bedroom, the cat was hitting the dog over the head with a toilet plunger.

"Okay, I'm all set," she said, slipping an earring into her ear.

"Gee, that didn't take long," I joked.

"Yeah, well I told you I was hungry," she said, missing the joke entirely.

She was wearing her new jeans, the red silk top, and black stiletto heels. The jeans appeared to be spray-painted on her gorgeous legs. She looked beautiful.

"You were worth the wait."

"Thanks," she said. "Now, let's get some food. My stomach is starting to rumble."

We took the elevator down to the ground floor. As we stepped outside, I looked up and down the street for anything or anyone suspicious. I didn't see a thing. We walked into the restaurant two doors down.

"Mmm, back for more?" The waitress from the night before said.

"Yes. Only this time we'd like to eat it here. You have a quiet table somewhere? Maybe towards the back?"

"I've just the thing," she said and led us into a small back room with four tables, two of which were occupied. "How is this?"

"Perfect," I said.

She pulled a chair out for Maddie, then handed us each a menu as we sat down. The menus were in English. "Something to drink? Wine, or perhaps a mixed drink?"

"A glass of wine would be nice," Maddie said.

The waitress handed her the drink menu and said she'd be back in a minute.

"Lots of wines," Maddie said. "What are you up for?"

"You know, you go ahead and order for the both of us. I'm fine with whatever you order."

Maddie ordered a bottle of something I couldn't remember, let alone pronounce. It was red and very delicious. We ordered dinner and a starter. We sat there nibbling and drinking wine for two hours, and we both finally started to dial down a bit and begin to relax.

After dinner, as the waitress began to clear our dishes, I asked, "Do you know a bar called Le Mondain? It's supposed to be in the ninth arrondissement."

"Oh, yes, a very nice spot. You are in the ninth arrondissement, now. The bar is only two or three of the blocks away. Very easy to get to." She proceeded to give us directions. I paid the bill and waited another while for Maddie to finish her glass of wine. She would raise the glass, and the moment the wine touched her lips, she would set the glass down. It was a good twenty minutes before we finally left.

Le Mondain was exactly where the waitress told us. Just a couple of blocks from our hotel. It was small and quiet. The room was maybe ten feet wide with a bar running along one wall. We sat at the end of the bar. As far away from the front window as we could get.

We ordered some wine, and when the barman delivered it, I asked for Jerome.

"That's me," he said with a smile.

"Your cousin, Matteo Martin in the US, is a friend of mine. He told us to come here," I said. I neglected to add that Matt was also a deadbeat, but after turning me on to this place, he was moving up in my estimation.

"Matteo? He is, how you say? A character."

"Yeah, that's pretty accurate. We wanted to travel out of Paris, and he thought you might be able to give us some ideas of places to go."

"What are you looking for?" He said and seemed to eye us suspiciously.

"Just some quiet place outside of Paris."

He thought about that for a long moment then said. "You know Château-Thierry?"

"Château-Thierry? The battlefield in the First World War?" My grand grandfather fought there in 1918. I didn't think Maddie would be into that.

"Yes, that's one of the things it's known for, but the other is Champagne. It is our Champaign region."

"I love Champagne," Maddie said.

"One moment," Jerome said. He walked to the far end of the bar, opened the door on a small refrigerator, and pulled out a chilled green bottle with gold foil wrapped around the neck of the bottle.

"Oh, Dev, I have to have some of that. I absolutely love Champagne," Maddie said.

Jerome set the bottle down in front of us. "You can see it is from our Champagne region. This brand, Pannier, they are located in Château-Thierry. They give wonderful tours. You can take the train from Paris to Château-Thierry. It's the perfect, how do you say, go away?"

"Get away?" I said.

"Yes, this is it. The perfect getaway."

"Can we try the Champagne?" Maddie said.

"I'm afraid once it's opened, you should drink it all."

"I can do that," Maddie said.

"Oh, I don't know, Maddie we . . ."

"We'll have the bottle. Give Mister Party Pooper here a small glass, and I'll have the rest."

Jerome looked at me.

"Better open it. It will only make my evening that much better."

"As you wish," Jerome said and flashed a big smile. He left and was back a moment later with an ice bucket and two crystal flutes that he set on the bar in front of us. He pulled the gold foil from the bottle. He aimed the bottle toward the back of the bar, placed his left hand around the neck of the bottle, and then began to twist the wire cage off the cork. He placed the cage on the bar. With his left hand still around the neck, he put his thumb on top of the cork and gently turned the bottle with his right hand, holding the bottom of the bottle.

"Is this going to shoot Champagne all over?" I said.

He shook his head. "Not if one does it properly."

The cork suddenly made a distinct popping sound, and the bottle was open. Not a drop of Champagne shot over the back of the bar. He filled our flutes, placed the bottle in the ice bucket, and said, "Enjoy."

Maddie grabbed her glass and took a large sip. "Mmm-mmm. Oh Dev, it's delicious. You have to try some."

I reluctantly picked up the Champagne flute, clinked glasses with her, and took a sip. To be honest, it was very good.

"This is a lot better than I expected."

"That's probably because it's not a ten-dollar bottle. I'm sure the stuff you've had in the past has just been rotgut," Maddie said and followed up with another hearty sip.

"Mmm-mmm, probably, now that you mention it. A couple of pals weddings and once in the bathtub with a friend."

"What kind did he have in the bathtub?"

"It wasn't a 'he', Maddie."

We finished the Champagne. The 'We' is a generous term. I sipped a glass and a half. Maddie finished the bottle. Her voice seemed to grow louder, and the laughs more frequent with each glass. When we left Le Mondain, she was feeling no pain.

Twenty-five

We began walking back to the hotel. We were maybe a block from Le Mondain with another two blocks to go. Just as we approached a gated entry to a courtyard, two figures stepped out of the shadows. One was very large. Maybe six-two, and the other a fireplug looking like Danny DeVito only with hair. Big Tony and Lurch Merda.

"Well, what do you know. Check this out, Lurch. Dev Haskell. Who knew? Talk about a small world, and here I thought this was a nice area," Big Tony said.

"Surprise, surprise. Hi guys," I said and kept moving, trying to walk around the two of them. Lurch blocked my way. I was about to step into the street when Lurch pulled me back. Maddie was a few steps behind me, humming a song no one would recognize and completely oblivious.

"Hi, guys? That's all you've got to say? We been looking for you, Haskell. Seems you and your gorgeous friend here have something we want."

"What the hell do you think you're doing? Not now," Maddie said.

"Hey, I don't know what you guys are talking about, but come 'mere," I said and signaled with my index finger for Big Tony to step closer. As he took a step toward me, I leaned in and caught him full force just under his chin with an uppercut from my right elbow. I heard his teeth crack together and saw his eyes roll up into his skull as he fell back onto the sidewalk. Lurch grabbed me by my shirt collar, but just as suddenly let go. I spun around to face him as Maddie delivered a second kick to his ribs. I heard an audible crack as he bent over and grabbed his side.

Maddie jumped about four feet, spun in midair, and delivered a stiletto heel to the side of his face. Lurch went down with a groan and collapsed on top of his unconscious brother. She landed on both feet and struck a Karate attack pose. Legs spread apart, leaning back slightly with one arm up at a right angle in front of her and the other palm up, in close to her chest.

Lurch coughed up blood onto Big Tony's shirt. I bent down, quickly searched him for a weapon, and found nothing. I rolled Lurch off his knocked out brother. Big Tony didn't move, and a little stream of blood dripped out of the corner of his mouth.

"What in the hell are you two doing here?"

Lurch groaned and coughed up more blood.

"You ain't looking so good right now, Lurch. Maybe next time, you won't forget your manners. Now, my friend and I are going back to our hotel. We're staying at the Hyatt in Paris. You want to talk, you can find us there. Just make sure you ask nice and polite next time."

Lurch gurgled something, but I couldn't make out what he was trying to say. A set of headlights turned onto the street and headed towards us. The taxi lights on top of the car were lit. I stepped into the street and raised my hand. The taxi stopped.

I opened the rear door and said to Maddie, "Come on, darling, or we're liable to be late."

Maddie gave me a quick look and backed away from the Merda brothers, saying something I couldn't hear and never taking her eyes off them. Once she was close to the taxi, she hurried into the back seat.

The taxi driver looked at the two bodies lying on the sidewalk. Lurch was in the process of rising up onto his knees. He was still bent over. His arms were wrapped around his sides, and he appeared to be in real pain.

"Trouble?" The driver asked in heavily accented English. He looked at me in the rearview mirror.

"They tried to rob us," I said.

He shook his head, muttered something in French, and took off down the street. I reached in my pocket and handed him a business card from our hotel. He muttered something else in French. Whatever he said didn't sound all that pleasant. He took the next left, and ten seconds later rolled to a stop in front of our hotel. The meter on the dashboard read four euros.

Oblivious Maddie slid out of the back seat. I handed a twenty euro note to the driver. When he pulled a wad of bills from his pocket, I said, "No. Keep the change," and shook my head.

He gave me a surprised look and muttered, "Merci."

Twenty-six

I hurried into the hotel and caught up with Maddie just as she stepped onto the elevator. The doors closed behind us, and she gave me a look. "Friends of yours? Who the hell were those guys?"

"I've sort of known about them for close to twenty years, and up until now, I've been successful at keeping my distance. They're not friends, and my guess is they were sent over here to grab that suitcase from you. They were on the same flight as we were. I saw them when I boarded the plane. I can't be a hundred percent sure, but I'm willing to bet they're working for Tubby. Where'd you learn Karate?"

"In my current business, you have to deal with all kinds. You said they work for Tubby?"

"It wouldn't surprise me."

"But how did they even know we were in there?"

"I'm trying to figure that part out. I've had my cell phone off. You haven't used yours, have you?"

"No, no. I haven't talked to anyone." Suddenly, she seemed more than a little nervous.

"Maddie, did you text anyone?"

"Text? Mmm-mmm, maybe a couple of friends. But it was just a text. I didn't talk to them."

"How many text messages did you send?" The elevator doors opened. Maddie quickly stepped off the elevator and hurried down the hall. I followed in close pursuit.

"Maddie, how many text messages have you sent?"

"Maybe just a few," she said and hurried around a corner.

"Did you send any from Le Mondain?"

"Not really. I mean, yeah, I guess so, but big deal, it was just two or three little ones with the picture of the Champagne bottle. God, what are you getting all worked up for? I sent them from the bathroom. So no one would know."

"No one would know? Maddie?"

She slipped her keycard into the lock, opened the door, and hurried into our suite. "What are you bitching about? I was in the bathroom. Who's going to know I sent a little text message?"

"That's how they found us, Maddie. They're tracking our cell phones. Is your phone still on?"

"Will you relax. I turned my phone off Mister Tight Control. Sorry I didn't ask for your permission to send a text message. God, what's the big deal?"

"Were you listening to me? It doesn't matter where you send it from. Even if you were in the bathroom, they could track your cellphone. Mine too, that's why I turned it off. I'm guessing they got a read in the area but couldn't pinpoint Le Mondain. That's why those two idiots were where they were. But if those two fools knew where we were, it's probably a sure bet that fat guy and his crew is wise to where we are, too. We're going to have to get out of here."

"Now?"

"Is your cellphone off?"

"I already told you."

"Show me, Maddie."

She flared her eyes at me as she pulled her cellphone from her back pocket and held it towards me. She pushed the button that would bring the screen up, but it remained off. "There, happy? I'm cut off from the world."

"Yeah, and we're both still alive. Leave that thing off. If you turn it on again, I'm going to take it from you."

Twenty minutes later, I was lying in bed when Maddie strolled out of the bathroom. She was naked and was swinging her thong around on her index finger as she strutted past. "Hey, Dev, like what you see?"

Apparently, she had calmed down. "Looking good, Maddie. Really great."

"Yeah, well, take a good long look cause that's all you're going to get tonight." She reached into her open suitcase and made a show of slipping into a pair of gym shorts. She took a t-shirt out of the suitcase and pulled it over her head. She slipped into the bed, took an extra pillow off the floor, and pushed it down between us. "Don't even think about it," she said. She rolled over on

her side, so her back was to me and pulled another pillow
over her head.

I woke in the middle of the night. Tiptoed over to
her side of the bed and grabbed her cellphone.

Twenty-seven

I woke Maddie up three separate times over the course of thirty minutes. Just now, I was on the phone with the front desk getting train schedules to Château-Thierry. The sun was threatening to rise. It wasn't quite five-thirty in the morning. I heard Maddie finally climb out of bed and head into the bathroom. The trains ran almost hourly throughout the day. The journey took about an hour and would run us less than twenty euros each for the tickets. As I hung up the phone, Maddie stepped out of the bathroom.

She was now wearing a white bathrobe over her gym shorts and t-shirt. She sat down on the couch across from me and crossed her arms. She still looked pissed off. "Who were you talking to?"

"I was just checking train times to Château-Thierry."

"And?"

"And they leave almost every hour. We can grab a taxi to the train station and get out of here just as soon as you're dressed."

"What's the rush? I need to take a shower, get dressed, might be nice to have something for breakfast." She stretched, groaned, and rubbed her eyes.

"What part of we're on borrowed time, do you not get?"

"I haven't sent anyone a text message if that's what you're bitching about."

I took a deep breath. "Maddie. I know you haven't sent a text message. But if they had the information that we were somewhere around here last night, don't you think it's probably a pretty safe bet they're checking all the hotels in the area? When they do get to this hotel, and they will, they're not going to be in the mood to knock politely on our door."

"Can I at least take a shower?"

"You can if you hurry. I plan on leaving in fifteen minutes."

"Fifteen?"

"Minutes. You can come with, or you can stay here. It doesn't matter to me. But I intend to get out of here, and I'm taking the money. The front desk is calling a taxi as we speak. It will be here in," I looked at the clock on the fireplace mantel. "It will be here in fourteen minutes, and I'm going to take it to the train station."

"Fourteen minutes? You gotta be kidding me. I can't get ready in that time."

"Not a problem." I glanced over at the clock again. "I need to get dressed and hurry downstairs. It's only thirteen minutes now." I stood and headed into the bedroom.

"Dev? Dev?" Maddie called and hurried into the bedroom. "Dev, I really do have to shower."

"Then you better get moving."

She shot me a killer look before she hurried into the bathroom. I leisurely got dressed and walked out to the front room and called the front desk.

"Bonjour," was how the phone was answered. I gave him our room number and said, "Would you order us a taxi, please? We'll be checking out in thirty minutes."

"But of course, sir. I'll have your paperwork waiting for you at the front desk."

I headed back into the bedroom. I dumped the fat guy's clothes on the floor. I lined all the shopping bags up on the edge of the bed and placed the metal briefcase in the empty suitcase. Maddie suddenly hurried out of the bathroom, rubbing a towel over her head. Her bathrobe hung open, and I stared for a long moment.

"How much time left?" she said, oblivious to my staring. She rummaged through a pink shopping bag and pulled out a thong and a bra. "Give me a minute, and I'll be ready to go."

"I'll wait for you in the other room," I said as I wheeled my suitcase into the front room.

Maddie hurried out of the bedroom ten minutes later. She was wheeling her suitcase and carrying the half dozen shopping bags.

"Maddie, I put all those shopping bags in your suitcase. Why did you take them out?"

"I've got about ten things going on right now. I needed some things since they probably won't let me on the train naked. If it's not too much trouble, maybe you could help." She dropped the shopping bags, pushed the suitcase toward me, pulled a hairbrush from her purse, and headed into the bathroom.

I opened her suitcase. The metal briefcase was in there along with the clothes she wore last night. I pulled the various items out of the shopping bag and packed them around the metal briefcase. It took all of a minute. I zipped the suitcase closed.

"Okay, princess. Time to go."

I heard her swear in the bathroom. A moment later, she stepped out. Her hair looked fine, and she had blue eye shadow on one eye.

"Do the other eye, and I'll see you downstairs. Don't be late."

She was already back in front of the bathroom mirror.

I wheeled both our suitcases down the hall and onto the elevator. At this early hour, there was no one in the hotel lobby other than the desk clerk and me. The sun was shining on the second story of the buildings across the street. It was not yet high enough to shine down on the sidewalk. As I folded our hotel receipt and placed it in a rear pocket, Maddie hurried around the corner.

"Perfect timing. The taxi should be here in just a moment."

"I thought you said it was waiting for us?"

"I thought it would be. Not to worry, we're all set to go."

"Oh, God! You are driving me crazy."

Twenty-eight

The Gare du Nord train station was a massive stone structure originally built in 1846 and located in the center of Paris. Three large arched windows rose up two and a half stories in the front of the structure. The windows had ten statues lined up across the front with seven more statues standing along the three-story roof line. Maddie and I grabbed our luggage from the taxi driver and stood and stared at the structure. All the locals just walked past hurrying toward their trains. They saw the place every day.

We purchased our tickets and made our way to platform eighteen. There were twenty-eight platforms in all. The place was jammed, and we had to go through security, showing our passports and tickets. Fortunately, they didn't check our luggage. When we arrived on the platform, the train was already being boarded. We had reserved seats and, surprisingly, found them without any problem. Twenty minutes later, the train departed. We picked up speed as we moved out of Paris and then rocketed across the country. Maddie pulled a red nylon bag from her suitcase and proceeded to work on her makeup. I stared out the window and watched the countryside fly by as the high-speed train zoomed along the tracks. It seemed in no time flat we were arriving in Château-Thierry.

The train pulled into the station, and the doors opened. We stepped off with maybe ten other people and found ourselves standing outside on an asphalt train platform beneath a metal roof. There was only one way out. We climbed up a long flight of stairs that led to a walkway running above a half dozen railroad tracks. We took the walkway to another set of stairs that led back down to ground level. I never did see an elevator. So much for handicapped access.

We walked through a small stucco building and, suddenly, found ourselves outside, standing in front of the station. There was an area marked for buses, but since we had no idea where we were going, there seemed no point in getting on a bus. As we stood with our suitcases looking around trying to get our bearings, Maddie said, "So now what?"

At that point, a taxi pulled up in front of us.

"Oh good, right on time," I said and waved at the driver like I'd been expecting him. He hopped out of the car, opened the trunk, and tossed our luggage in. He held the door for Maddie, and I entered on the opposite side.

As he slid back behind the wheel, he hit the meter, which automatically registered a three euro fee. "Where are you going?" he said in accented English.

"Hotel," I said and shrugged, indicating I had absolutely no idea.

He nodded and took off. Apparently, people with no idea was just an everyday occurrence. We drove through town, across a river into an older part of the town, and navigated through a series of narrow streets, up a steep hill to a massive, white, four-story hotel that overlooked the town. We paid the fare and rolled our luggage into the lobby. Amazingly, the Hotel Ile de France was part of the Best Western chain.

We booked a room on the third floor. As hotel rooms go, it was nice. It overlooked the front entrance, a little patio area where people were sitting in the shade, finishing what looked like breakfast. The town was spread out before us below the hill.

Maddie looked out at the people eating and said, "You think we might be able to fit some form of nourishment into your schedule?"

"Hey, look. I know I've been a pain, but after our run-in with those two idiots last night, we needed to get out of Paris. Now that we're here, we can hopefully begin to take it easy. Nothing crazy, but let's plan on keeping a low profile and enjoy ourselves. I've been thinking. It would probably be a good idea to book different flights home. It's not like we're hurting for money to pay for a flight. We could probably even book first class."

"Different flights?"

"Remember, since those guys grabbed your luggage, they probably have your flight information. Wouldn't surprise me if they were waiting for you to get on that flight. Now that I think about it, it would probably make a lot of sense to fly out of some other city instead of Paris. That way, we can avoid them completely."

"Well then, why are we even here?"

"Because there was a pretty good chance they would have been looking for us on trains going to London, Frankfurt, or Amsterdam. They're not going to be expecting us to travel here to Château-Thierry. Now, we can take it easy for a day or two and leisurely, decide where we're going to fly out of."

"So, does this mean you're finally going to be in a good mood?"

"Maddie, I've been in a good mood. That doesn't mean we shouldn't be cautious. So before you ask, no, you're not going to text people. You saw what happened last night with your text messages."

"I don't know why I'm getting blamed just because some creeps you knew decided to cause a problem. Besides, I only sent a few text messages."

"A few? You told me three."

"Mmm, I may have forgotten about a couple of the others. Anyway, let's not go there. How about breakfast? Maybe, we could eat it out there?" She nodded at the patio overlooking the town.

"Sounds like a plan. Come on, let's grab something to eat and check this place out. They're supposed to have a pool, a gym, and a sauna. Maybe we can check out the town after we eat. You go on downstairs and get a table. I'm going to use the bathroom, and then I'll be down."

"Okay, see you out there on the patio," Maddie said.

Twenty-nine

We sat out on the patio in the sun and enjoyed our breakfast. Maddie had a small bowl of fruit and a croissant. I had fried eggs, pancakes, a caramel roll, and a side order of bacon.

"Are you expecting someone to join us?" Maddie said, looking at the various plates spread around me.

"Hey, watching over you and keeping us safe builds up an appetite."

"Believe me. I don't need watching. I've made it this far on my own."

"You said you dropped out of school in the eleventh grade?"

"Yeah. What I didn't tell you was I got my GED, and I've finished up four semesters at the U. I'm going for a teaching degree."

"Teaching? You mean like in a classroom? With kids?"

"Don't sound so surprised. One of the things that happened after I dropped out is it quickly became pretty clear that if I didn't want to work at some dead-end job for the rest of my life, I had to get an education. A woman in my building got me thinking about going into teaching. I want to teach special needs kids. I'd like to help them."

"Seriously?"

"What do you mean by that?"

"I didn't mean anything. Well, other than I'm surprised. I didn't have you figured for someone who wanted to be a teacher."

"You mean because I'm dancing?"

"No. No, I didn't mean it that way."

"Yeah, you did. Everyone thinks because I'm dancing that I'm a slut and probably a coke head too."

"No, I wasn't thinking that. I just—"

"Dev, if you didn't think that you'd be the first person who didn't. Of course, no one is interested in the fact I don't have any college debt, and I have money in the bank. They only want to know what I do to get the tips and what my stage name is."

"Tubby know you're going to school?"

"He might. Not that it's any of his business. He's never asked if that's what you mean. For the hours involved, I make very good money dancing. And yes, I'd be the first one to admit that a lot of the girls have some real issues. Not my problem. I perform. I get paid, and I go to school."

"Why do you think he chose you to go to Paris."

"Well, initially, I thought it was because he was just being nice."

"Tubby Gustafson?"

"Yeah, I know. Call it a learning experience. After what we've been through. The whole suitcase debacle. Last night with Big Tony and Lurch. I'm beginning to think he chose me because I don't have any family. I don't have a boyfriend. If something happened to me, I don't know that anyone would even care."

I figured she'd probably be a pretty good teacher if she already remembered Big Tony and Lurch's names. "I'd care."

"Oh, thanks. That's nice. But you know what I mean. No parents wondering where I was, no boyfriend tagging along. You know?"

"Yeah. I guess I get it. Hey, as long as we're here, Miss Higher Education, we can poke around the ruins of the local castle. It's called Château de Château-Thierry."

"And you know this how?"

"You kidding? I'm a font of useless information. We can check out the ruins, and then this afternoon, I'm thinking there might be a Champagne tasting in our immediate future."

"Oh, Dev, you mean it?"

"Yeah. We have to. That Pannier Champagne you really liked last night at Le Mondain. Jerome said they have a tasting room here. I think we should check it out. I guess it's a big tourist attraction, and well, we're tourists from here on in."

Maddie inhaled the rest of her croissant and pushed the remainder of her fruit bowl toward me. "Here you finish this. I want to save room for the Champagne."

I looked at the half stack of pancakes I had left. No guts, no glory. I dug in.

Thirty

We grabbed some cash from the briefcase and took a taxi to a currency exchange next to the local tourist office. The hundred dollar bills were crisp, and the guy behind the counter looked at us and said, "Very new."

"Fresh from our bank," I said and smiled.

He ran a marker over the serial numbers on each hundred dollar bill. Once again, all the bills passed muster, and we got a stack of twenty euro notes in exchange. I handed half the euros to Maddie.

The Château of Château-Thierry was actually the ruins of a castle from hundreds of years back. I was enjoying walking around the grounds looking at the towers originally built for archers and checking out the massive stone walls. Maddie seemed bored after about fifteen minutes.

"You don't seem to be enjoying this, Maddie."

"No, it's okay. I guess if you like wrecked stuff. It's just that how many stone walls do you have to see before they all start to run together?"

"What if you end up at a school that wants you to be the history teacher?"

"Then I'll teach stuff that's interesting. You know, like what the people were like. Why they had to build the castle in the first place. What they ate. Where they lived. Great to think about royalty, but the thing about royalty is they needed worker bees like you and me to be able to live like royalty."

"Well, what do you know?"

"What?"

"I think you'll make a good history teacher. Or, for that matter, a good teacher, no matter what the subject."

"Thanks. Now I'm wondering if we should get to the Champagne place and study their product before it closes."

"Closes? It's not even noon yet."

She glanced at her watch. "It's eleven-fifty."

"Oh, forgive me. Only eight hours left, I guess we better hurry. Come on. We can grab a taxi and head over there."

Literally, Maddie skipped out of the castle grounds and headed toward the taxi stand. The trip to the Pannier reception center took less than ten minutes, and only that long because we had to wait for three separate traffic lights.

The building was a two-story white stucco structure on a hill at the edge of town. Gold letters at the top of the building read CHAMPAGNE and below that in letters twice as large the name, PANNIER. The taxi pulled up to the front door, and Maddie hopped out while I paid the driver. She had already stepped inside by the time I climbed out of the cab.

There was a sales area offering all sorts of products. Not only bottles of Champagne but hats, t-shirts, shopping bags, jackets, you name it. Maddie was in front of the tour counter and waved me over as I looked around, trying to find her.

"Dev, the next tour starts in just a couple of minutes."

Behind the counter, a screen flashed several different images of vineyards, all sorts of distilling equipment, and caves with all kinds of stored bottles of Champagne and wooden casks stacked on top of one another.

"You want to do the tour?"

"Well, yeah. Why else would we be here?"

"I was thinking we were going to taste Champagne."

"That too, but let's do the tour first," she said and stepped aside so I could pay.

"Okay, okay." I paid for our tickets. We each got a set of headphones with a half dozen language options. Fortunately, one of the options was English, and we started our tour. We looked out the windows at acres of vineyards. We wandered past all sorts of fermentation equipment and through miles of underground caverns filled with wooden casks and bottles in various storage facilities. After more than an hour, we made our way to the tasting room. I heard more about Champagne than I would ever remember.

The tasting began with a series of four small Champagne flutes. Each flute tasted slightly different. Maddie had booked us on the premium tour, and we gradually tasted our way up to the more expensive Champagnes. It seemed the more expensive the Champagne, the more she seemed to love it. By the end of the tasting, I was giving my sample to Maddie. She appeared to be feeling no pain at this stage.

Eventually, we made our way back toward the entry area. Maddie purchased a baseball cap, a t-shirt, a shopping bag, and three bottles of Champagne.

"You sure that's enough?" I said.

"Not to worry, I can come back tomorrow if I want to."

As we headed for the door, I casually looked through the tinted glass entry. There was a grey vehicle parked just across the street at the edge of a parking lot. The car was facing us. Two rough-looking characters sat in the front seat, and the car was leaning decidedly to the left. I immediately thought of the fat man on the plane, Ali Debauche. The man with the million-dollar suitcase.

"Hold on a second, Maddie," I said and pulled her back from the door.

"What is it?"

"Remember when we left the first hotel, and I told you the fat man from the airport was racing up the street past us?"

"Yeah?"

"I think that's him right across the street. I'm pretty sure that's the same car from the other day. See the way it's leaning. The fat guy is probably in the back seat on the right-hand side. How in the hell did they—?"

"Umm, I might have sent a text before we left Paris."

"What?" I said it loud enough that a number of heads turned.

"I'm sorry, Dev. I didn't think there would be a problem because we weren't going to be in Paris."

"Maddie, I took the battery out of your phone last night. How in the hell could you text someone."

"I know you did, but I always carry a spare. You know, just in case." She shrugged like it was no big deal.

"A spare cell phone battery? Oh great. That worked out well," I said and looked out at the carload of thugs across the street.

"Well, maybe they won't spot me. After all, I've got my new hair."

At that moment, it wasn't Maddie I was worried about. A group of about a dozen noisy college students headed toward the door. "Fall in with these kids and walk with them. If the car doesn't follow you, I'll deal with these guys and see you back at the hotel. As soon as you're out of sight, grab a taxi and take it to the hotel. Stay in our room. Don't go anywhere."

"What about you?"

"I just told you. I'll deal with these guys."

"But, Dev, I—"

"Just do it, and please, for God's sake, do not text anyone."

"You sure you can—"

"Maddie, get going with these kids." The group was passing us. It sounded like they were all speaking Italian, but I couldn't be sure. Maddie sort of wiggled her way into the middle of the group. Two of the guys backed off a half step and appraised her from the rear. They elbowed one another, chuckled, and one of them moved his hands indicating, some of Maddie's finer points. I couldn't understand a word they said, but I had a pretty good idea of what they were referring to. The group took a left out the door and headed down the hill.

Thirty-one

I waited a good five minutes, but the car across the street never moved. I took a deep breath and headed out the door. Heads turned on the two guys in the front seat, and they appeared to say something. I looked both ways before I crossed the street and headed for the parking lot behind them. The car was running, and as I approached, both front doors slowly opened. I headed toward the guy on the driver's side, trying to make it look like I had a car parked somewhere behind them.

"Pardon, Monsieur," he said as he stepped out and began to reach beneath his jacket.

He wasn't fully upright, as I slowly began to raise my hands. I suddenly hopped on my left leg and kicked the door with my right leg. His pistol bounced down on the ground as the door frame caught him at the base of his nose. The door sort of bounced open, as the guy bent forward holding his nose. I charged the door and shouldered it, cracking his head between the door and the door frame. His eyes appeared to cross, and he began to slide along the side of the car. I picked up the pistol just before his body hit the ground.

I crouched down and moved to the back of the car. In chrome letters on the trunk was the word 'Citroën.' The fat guy began yelling something from the back seat. I looked under the car and watched a pair of feet move to the front of the vehicle. I crouched around to the side of the car and headed toward the open passenger door. The car suddenly rocked from side to side as the fat guy oozed across the rear seat. I leaned in through the open door and pointed the pistol at him. Fatty looked at me, and his eyes grew wide. "You."

"Tell him to drop the gun," I said.

He didn't move.

"Tell him to drop the gun," I said and pulled the hammer back on the pistol.

Fatty shouted something in French, and the other guy suddenly appeared at the back of the car. He was short and stocky. He had dark hair, not quite shaved but close enough. There was a scar above his right eye that made him look like he had two eyebrows on that side of his face.

"Tell him to very carefully toss his gun on the driver's seat."

"We should talk, Monsieur Hassle," he said in heavily accented English.

"Now's not a good time. What you should do is tell him to carefully toss his pistol on the driver's seat, now. I should warn you. I'm very nervous right now, this gun is pointed at you, and it may go off."

He seemed to think about that for a second or two before he called out in French.

The guy at the back of the car said something, and Fatty responded, this time sounding a little louder and a lot more direct. The guy stepped to the side of the vehicle and tossed his pistol onto the driver's seat. Still on the ground, the driver groaned and moved a leg.

"Get your ass out of the car," I said to Fatty.

"Yes. Yes, I'm moving. All right, please, remain calm. Now, Monsieur, I believe you have something that belongs to me. I merely want it back, and there'll be no problems. You and the girl will be free to go. I'll even give you some money. We can be friends. Yes?"

"I don't think so. Get out of the car."

"Please, I beg you to think about this. I'm giving you an option. Yes? Otherwise, I fear you have no idea the trouble you will find yourself in, Monsieur Hassle. Please, take a moment and think."

"Get out of the car. I'm not going to tell you again."

He shook his head as he opened the door, turned sideways, planted his feet on the ground, and groaned as he stood. The car rocked side to side for a moment once the three hundred plus pounds stood in the parking lot.

I kept the gun on both of them and hurried around the front of the car. "Pick your pal up and start moving toward the back of the lot. You so much as look back, and all bets are off."

"Think about this, please, what you are doing. You are making a big mistake. A very big mistake. Please, think."

"The only mistake here is you trying to follow us. Now, get him to his feet and start moving back." I waved the pistol at Fatty and his friend standing at the rear of their car. The guy on the ground groaned and moved his legs.

"Monsieur Hassle, please, you are not—"

"Last chance, before all three of you end up in the hospital, and the police are involved. Now get moving."

Fatty said something to the thug standing next to him. The guy gave him a look but didn't say anything. He reached down and groaned as he helped his pal to his feet. Blood was running from the man's nose and had dripped along either side of his mouth. There was a straight line welt across his forehead, maybe four inches long with a purple line down the center. He raised the injured man's arm over his shoulder, and they turned and headed toward the back of the parking lot.

Fatty was saying something as they moved, but I couldn't hear it and wouldn't have understood it anyway. When they were maybe twenty feet away, I slid into the driver's seat of their car, put the car in drive and took off. For the first time, I noticed the half dozen people standing across the street in front of the Pannier Champagne building staring wide-eyed, with their mouths hanging open. I took a right and sped down the street.

Thirty-two

It wasn't the most direct route, but I eventually made it back to the hotel in the Citroën. I screeched to a stop in front of the hotel and charged up to our room. As I stepped off the elevator, I ran into Maddie, hurrying down the hall with her suitcase.

"Dev?"

"Maddie? What are you doing?"

"I, I didn't know if you were going to be okay. Didn't know what might have happened to you. I was, umm, going to take a taxi to the police station and tell them what happened. Are you okay? Was that the bad guys? Did they follow you?"

"Yes, yes, and no. I'm fine. They didn't follow me, but I think it might be a good idea if we checked out here and left town. Like right away."

"You gotta be kidding?"

"No, I'm deadly serious."

"Are we going back to Paris?"

"I'm not sure where we're going. But I know one thing, it's not gonna be Paris."

"What happened? Where are those guys in the car?"

"Right now, I would say there's a pretty good chance they're looking for us. Hopefully, they don't know we're staying here. But let's not press our luck." I nodded at her suitcase. "You pack the briefcase?"

"Umm, yeah. I didn't know what else to do, and I was afraid they might be coming here."

"Yeah, well, I'm not so sure they aren't headed this way. So, let's get the hell out of here. Come on back to the room while I pack."

"I was thinking, maybe I'd check us out."

I thought about that for a second. "Okay, good idea. Go ahead and do that. I'll join you down there in a couple of minutes."

She smiled, pressed the button for the elevator, and the door immediately opened. As she started to step onto the elevator, I said, "Hold on a second, Maddie. Give me that luggage, and I'll bring it down with mine. No point and having it exposed any more than we have to."

"Oh, it'll be okay. I'll wait for you at the front desk."

"The way the day is going, why take the chance? I'll be down in five minutes."

The elevator door started buzzing, signaling it had been open too long. Maddie's suitcase, with the briefcase and money inside, was standing in front of the electric eye on the elevator door. I grabbed hold of the handle and wheeled it back into the hallway. "See you down there in a few minutes," I said just as the door closed on a frustrated looking Maggie.

I rolled the suitcase back down the hall to our room. It took me about two minutes to throw everything into my suitcase and do a quick check in the room for anything missed. I opened Maddie's suitcase checking to be sure the briefcase was in there. It was. I rummaged around her clothes and makeup bag looking for her cellphone but didn't find it. I hurried out of the room and back down the hall. Maddie was standing at the front desk in the process of checking out. I wheeled our suitcases out to the Citroën and put them in the trunk. Maddie's was much heavier because of the briefcase. I hurried back into the hotel. Maddie was in the process of folding the receipt from the hotel and slipping it into her back pocket.

"All set?" I said just as she turned around.

"Yeah. We're checked out. Did you already call a taxi?"

"No, come on," I said and headed out the door.

"No? Well, what did you do with the suitcases? You didn't leave them out front, did you?" She was looking around the lobby, her head racing left and right, growing more frantic by the second.

"Maddie, come on?"

"Where are they?" She gave a disgusted groan and quickly followed me out of the door. "After all we've been through this is really stupid of you to—"

I clicked the unlock button on the car keys. The signal lights blinked, and the horn chirped.

"You rented a car?"

"Not exactly, but nothing's too good for you, Maddie. Come on, hop in, and let's get out of here."

"I kind of hate to go. I was beginning to like this town."

"Yeah, but unfortunately, we have some unwanted acquaintances looking for us so, we need to hightail it out of here."

"Where are we going?"

"Hop in. Oh, and give me your cellphone, please."

She shot me a look.

"Maddie, if those thugs waiting for us across the street at Pannier weren't enough of a warning, I don't know what will be. You could have gotten us killed."

"I didn't text them, Dev."

"Well, I sure as hell didn't. You were the one sending text messages that they were most likely able to trace. You think they just happened to be in front of that Champagne place and just happened to park where they did because they liked the place?"

"Yeah, sure. That's right, Dev. Go ahead and blame me. Apparently, it must be my fault. Everything else is."

"I'm not trying to be a jerk, but there's a lot of money involved, and these guys aren't going to be nice about it. Now give me your phone, or I'm going to leave you here."

She frowned, reached into her purse, grabbed the phone, and then shoved it at me as if it were a knife. "And you don't have to try to be a jerk, because you are a jerk. Asshole. There, happy?"

"Just about," I said. I looked at the phone and pressed a button. The screen lit up. She had it turned on. "You gotta be kidding me. You have this thing turned on? You got a death wish or something?"

"Sorry, Crabby. Guess I just forgot."

"Ahh, relax, it's okay. I held the button down on the side of the phone. After a few seconds, the words 'Power Off' appeared in red on the screen. I touched the screen. The phone turned off. I placed it in my right hand and tossed it over the line of cars parked at the edge of the parking lot. The phone landed in the field just beyond the cars, bounced once, and disappeared in the weeds."

"Oh my God. Dev? Are you nuts? What did you do that for?" She headed for the phone.

I climbed in behind the wheel and started the engine. Maddie stopped about ten feet from the car. She looked at me and back to the field where her phone had landed. I began to pull away.

"Dev, wait, wait," she said and hurried back to the car. I accelerated before she'd closed her door. "You know, you can be a real asshole," she said as she buckled up.

"Yeah, you mentioned that. And you can really be stupid. You pull another stunt like that, and I'm leaving you, no matter where we are."

Her eyes flared, and she looked like she was about to say something but suddenly thought better of it. She settled into the seat, crossed her arms, and stared straight ahead. Her cheeks were crimson, and I figured the best move would be not to say anything. We headed out of Château-Thierry and onto the A4 highway. A little over an hour later, we were on the outskirts of the city of Reims.

"How does Reims sound?"

"Humph," Maddie said. Her arms were still crossed and she continued to stare straight ahead.

"It's supposed to be a big Champagne center. Lots of tastings."

"Okay, it sounds a little better. Maybe," she said, but she still wouldn't look at me.

Thirty-three

I pulled into the parking lot at a train station on the outskirts of the city.

"We're taking a train somewhere? I thought we were staying here in Reims," Maddie said, ready to settle back into her bad attitude.

"Relax, and let's grab the luggage. We're staying in the city. I just wanted to ditch the car."

"Ditch the car? But why? We just got here. You plan on walking everywhere?"

"I plan on not being followed. I'm sure by now whoever this belongs to, presumably that fat guy, figures we left Château-Thierry. There's a pretty good chance he's listed this car as stolen. Maybe even told the cops I assaulted him and took it by force, which isn't too far from the truth. Anyway, we're on borrowed time with this set of wheels. We'll leave it here at the station. Hopefully, they'll figure we took a train somewhere and give up trying to find us. Come on, let's grab a taxi, find a hotel, and relax."

I left the keys in the ignition. Maddie pulled her makeup bag out of the trunk. I grabbed the two suitcases, stacked mine on top of Maddie's, and headed toward the taxi stand in front of the station. We walked up to the first taxi in the line. The driver was leaning against the side of the cab, chatting with the driver from the cab parked behind him. It must have been a slow day.

"Parlez-vous, English?" I said.

"Yes, a little," he replied and nodded. He was exactly what you might expect a French taxi driver to look like. A bit heavy. In need of a shave. He wore blue jeans, a khaki shirt, and a soft cap on his head. He reached in through the driver's window and pressed a button. The lid on the trunk rose about four inches.

I wheeled the suitcases around to the back of the car. He pulled mine off the top and set it in the trunk. He took hold of Maddie's, shot me a look, grunted, and tossed it into the trunk after hoisting it up on his hip.

"Sorry that one's so heavy," I said.

If he understood me, he didn't acknowledge it. He hurried around to the side of the car and opened the door for Maddie. "Morceau de cul," he said and smiled. He motioned with his hand for Maddie to get into the back seat.

"Mmm-mmm, manners," she said and shot me a look suggesting I didn't have any.

I opened the other door and slid in. The driver slid behind the wheel and then turned and raised his eyebrows at me.

"Umm, hotel?" I said.

He nodded, said a long something in French, and looked at me as if anticipating an answer. I smiled, nodded back, and we took off. We raced through streets for the next ten minutes, missing pedestrians and parked cars by fractions of an inch. We took a fast, hard right and suddenly drove into a park. Maddie saw the sign first, Parc de Champagne.

"This sounds okay," she said, looking out at gorgeous trees and up ahead a three-story stone building with pillars in front and second-floor balconies. "Oh, wow, I wonder who lives there?"

"Domaine Les Crayeres," the driver said and headed for the circular drive. He barely missed the large stone planter filled with flowers in the middle of the drive and screeched to a stop in front of the building.

"Hotel?" I said.

"Oui." He nodded and popped the lid on the trunk.

"I guess this is our stop, Maddie."

"Oh, this is going to be special."

"I thought you might like it."

"Yeah, nice try, but you're just as surprised as me. So get out."

I paid our fare and climbed out of the taxi. The driver hoisted our luggage out of the trunk, smiled, jumped back into the cab, and sped off.

"Well, let's check it out," I said, and we headed for the front door. I hadn't taken three steps when the double doors opened, and a guy in a black uniform hurried out and took the luggage from me.

"Please, allow me, Monsieur," he said, taking hold of the suitcases. I didn't argue. We followed him up the walk to the entrance. He stepped back and let us go ahead of him. I held the door for Maddie.

"Oh, wow. Check this place out. I don't believe it. Dev, look at this place. It's like a palace or something." Maddie stood in the lobby with her mouth open, gazing at the paneled walls and the elegant furniture arranged around two elaborate fireplaces.

"Sure you like it? We can go somewhere else if you want to. Probably a Holiday Inn somewhere around here."

"Shut up and check us in," she said, still looking around. She kept turning, completing a full circle staring at the lobby. Our luggage was now up at the front desk, where a smiling woman waited to check us in. Probably not the first time she had people arrive and become immediately overwhelmed the moment they stepped through the front door.

I hurried up to the front desk.

"Good day, Monsieur. You have a reservation. Yes?"

"Umm, no, I'm sorry we do not. We just arrived, and our taxi man gave you an excellent recommendation. Hopefully, you have a room available."

"But of course. We do have one still available. Our Prestige Suite."

The Prestige Suite. At any other time in my life, I would have thought I was about to be taken. But, right now, with a suitcase full of cash and no way we could be found . . . "That sounds perfect. We'd like it for two nights."

"Two nights. But of course, Monsieur. If you would be so kind as to fill this out and sign at the bottom." She slid a registration form across the marble counter to me and handed me a fountain pen. This wasn't some nineteen cent ballpoint but a heavy, silver fountain pen. I carefully wrote down bogus information, lied about my address in the states, and scribbled a fake signature. "I would prefer to pay in cash if that's all right."

"By all means. Not a problem, Monsieur. I'll still need a credit card to run," she flashed a quick smile suggesting there would be no further discussion. I handed her my credit card then crossed my fingers it wouldn't be denied. Surprisingly, my card went through.

"Very good, Monsieur. Raphael will now show you to your room," she said and slapped the top of the reception counter bell. It dinged.

Raphael took one step over and said, "Oui?"

How could he not know what he was supposed to do? For that matter, did she really have to ring the bell? He was standing right next to me, ogling Maddie while she continued to stare at the antique furniture and the fireplaces.

The receptionist said a brief sentence in French, which probably amounted to, "Take the luggage up to their room."

Thirty-four

O ur room, the 'Prestige Suite,' was red. I mean virtually everything but the ceiling and the fireplace was red. Gorgeous red silk wallpaper. A red couch in front of a black fireplace. Red silk sheets, six pillows in red silk cases, a red duvet draped across a king-size bed with a red leather headboard. The ceiling was ten feet high, white and edged with elaborate plaster trim that looked a hundred years old. The gigantic paned windows, there were two, looked out onto a sculpted lawn and the park beyond. Embroidered red curtains framed the windows and were pulled back by red silk ties attached to brass holders.

"God, it's like a high priced whore house," Maddie said and leaped onto the bed. She bounced a half dozen times in an effort to touch the ceiling. Fortunately, she didn't collapse the bed. On her last jump, she raised her legs and bounced onto the bed. As she landed, she snuggled her head between two of the silk covered pillows. An antique wood desk sat off to the side in a corner with a gold chair upholstered in red striped cushions and positioned at an angle.

I strolled into the bathroom and flicked on the light. Everything was white tiles with the exception of the cast iron tub, which looked like it could accommodate four adults comfortably. A glass-enclosed shower stood in the corner. Two white robes with gold embroidered crests over the left breast hung from antique wooden hangers. A gold tray of soaps, shampoo, and body creams rested on the white marble vanity between the two sinks. The mirror over the sinks was beveled and hung in an ornate antique gold frame.

I strolled back into the bedroom. Maddie had kicked her shoes off and was in the process of pulling down her jeans.

"Can I help?"

"It's so lovely, Dev. I just want to climb under the covers for a minute. Silk sheets. Can you believe it?"

"I think we've earned it. We've been dodging bad guys for the past couple of days in Paris. We can take it easy here and then fly back to the states from Amsterdam or Munich, or even Madrid."

"God. Can you imagine living like this all the time?"

"Actually, no, I can't. But let's not go there. I'd rather enjoy the next couple of days."

She tossed her blouse on the gold chair in front of the antique desk. She made a show of unhooking her bra before tossing it in the general direction of the chair. Her thong followed as she kicked it towards the chair. She took her time posing in front of the mirror before slipping between the silk sheets.

"How is it?" I asked as a look of pure pleasure washed over her face.

"Mmm-mmm, it's absolutely wonderful. Maybe you should think about joining me in here."

Thirty minutes later, we both laid back and took a breather.

"That was fantastic, the absolute best," Maddie said.

"Thank you."

"I didn't mean you, Dev. Well, yeah, you were okay, I guess. But for a while, it was like being a real-life princess, and I could have the pick of any guy I wanted."

"But you can do that on just about any day."

"This is a little higher class than the back seat in someone's car or the ratty couch in some guy's efficiency apartment."

I decided not to go there.

She rolled over on her side and faced me. "Mind if I ask you a question? What, exactly, are we going to do with all this cash?"

"Seriously? You want to discuss that now? Here? After we just had a fantastic—"

"I just asked a simple question."

"Okay, yeah, maybe your right. We're going to bring it back to the states. Bring it back to St. Paul, and we're going to give it to your pal, Tubby Gustafson."

"But we've spent some of the money."

"And you can tell him the truth. You had to go on the run to hide from that fat guy and those thugs the other night who wanted to steal the money. Tell him you risked your life to get as much of it back to him as you could. In fact, I'd suggest you tell him you maybe wouldn't be opposed to some sort of a reward."

"What are you going to do?"

"I'm going to agree with everything you tell him."

"But the money we've spent. It's not—"

"The money we've spent over the past couple of days doesn't even make a dent in the close to a million bucks you're going to be handing over to him. Believe me, you're doing him a big favor. Right now, we've eliminated our biggest problem, those thugs trying to get the money. Even after Tubby sent his own guys over here, Big Tony and Lurch. How are they going to find us? You're not texting anyone, are you?"

"No, and don't remind me. I'm still pissed off you threw my phone away."

"Maddie, think of it as a golden opportunity. When we get back in the states, you can take some of Tubby's cash and buy yourself whatever phone you want. Get the best one out there, maybe prepay it for a year and get a fancy case, too. You can get whatever you want. Somehow I think you'll survive being off the radar for the next seventy-two hours."

"I'm not so sure."

"You're just going through withdrawal. I honestly don't get it. You text your friends back and forth, back and forth. Wouldn't it just be a hell of a lot easier to call

whoever it is you're texting and get an answer to whatever your question is?"

"It doesn't work like that."

"Yeah, and that's another problem."

"You're ruining the moment, Dev."

"You brought it up."

"I got a better idea," she said and pulled me on top
of her.

Thirty-five

We took a long nap, grabbed a shower, had a glass of wine in front of the fireplace while wearing the hotel's thick white robes with the gold embroidered crests. A force of habit, Maddie arranged her robe in a revealing position while she paged through a hotel brochure. Despite our earlier afternoon activities, I was perfectly content to sip wine and stare.

"Have you given any thought to dinner?" She said.

"Not really, I'm still in the recovery mode from our workouts."

She smiled and said, "You seemed to enjoy yourself. I don't know about you, but I certainly worked up an appetite. It looks like they've got a very nice restaurant right here in the hotel. Would it be okay if we just had dinner here?"

"Yeah, fine with me." I envisioned a place with booths and maybe a jukebox. A couple of cheeseburgers with fries, maybe some onion rings, and a shake. It all sounded perfect to me.

"Mmm-mmm. Although, I'm not sure I have anything appropriate to wear."

"What's wrong with your jeans and that blouse. You look great in them."

"Dev," she said, leaning forward and exposing herself as she handed me the brochure. "Look at these pictures. Everyone is dressed up. The place has linen tablecloths and lit candles on the tables. Let me just run out and get a different blouse. I think we passed a couple of shops on the way into the park."

"Those pictures in the brochure are probably just an advertising gimmick. They're meant to get you prepared to pay exorbitant prices. You sure you want to go clothes shopping?"

"Don't worry. You won't have to come. In fact, it might be a good idea if you just stayed here and rested up. I just might be looking for some more personal attention after dinner," she said and raised her eyebrows.

Suddenly eating in the fancy hotel restaurant was beginning to sound like a pretty good idea.

"You want me to go with you?"

"Oh, thanks, but I know how much you'd enjoy that, like not at all. There's an exercise area with a pool and a sauna, and it has an area around the pool where you can sit in the sun if you're bored with this room. It's on the back page of that brochure."

I turned to the back page. There was a photo of an outdoor pool with three separate couples lying on lounge chairs. The women were gorgeous and topless. The guys appeared to be drinking beer and not paying attention.

"Yeah, maybe a light workout would be just the thing after driving here."

"Okay," she said and was suddenly on her feet. Before I knew it, she was in the process of pulling her jeans on and stepping into her shoes. "I won't be long. Just going to look for a top. If you're not in the room when I get back, I'll go down to that exercise area."

"Yeah, I'll probably swim some laps down there. I'll call and make a reservation for dinner around eight in the restaurant. Sound okay?"

"That sounds perfect. Thanks, Dev. I won't be long."

"Take all the time you need," I said.

I watched her hurry out the door with her purse slung over her shoulder. Amazing someone can get that excited about going shopping. I hated it. I go into a store with a list, get whatever I needed, as quickly as possible, and get the hell out. The more I thought about it, the more I wondered. Would she buy a phone? Did she somehow take the briefcase?

I hopped off the couch and opened her suitcase. The briefcase was there. I opened it. It looked relatively untouched. Even if she did purchase a phone, she'd be issued a new number, so how would anyone be able to trace it back to us? I picked up the brochure, opened it to the page with the topless women sunning themselves on the lounge chairs, and decided a swim was just what I needed. I took the briefcase and hid it behind the red silk drapes.

Thirty-six

The workout area had a service counter with a young couple in hotel uniforms standing behind it. As I stepped into the room, they both smiled and said, "Good afternoon." Once again, I was amazed they could determine I didn't speak French before I uttered a word.

"Good afternoon," I replied. "I wanted to see about using the pool, but I'm afraid I don't have a swimsuit."

"Not a problem, sir. We have some you can rent, or if you would prefer, we have some in the counter down here for purchase."

I didn't have to think very long. "I think I'd like to purchase one."

"But of course," he said and smiled.

He walked to the end of the counter. As I approached, he slid open a door on the back of the glass case. He pulled out four swimsuits, all a dark burgundy and all looking like boxer shorts. The swimsuits were different sizes. One was clearly too small. Two were too large. Fortunately, one seemed about right.

"I'll take this one."

"Very well, and you wish to change here?"

"Yeah."

"But of course, the men's locker room is just through that door. If you wish, I can charge this to your room, sir."

"Yes, if you would, please." I gave him my room number. He handed me a locker key and a towel. I headed into the men's locker room. I changed quickly, draped the towel over my shoulder, and headed for the pool.

The weather was sunny and warm, thank God it wasn't the dreadfully stifling Midwest humid heat I half expected. Unfortunately, I was the only person in the outside pool area. I draped my towel over the back of a lounge chair and walked to the deep end of the pool. I dove in, swam a length, and decided, that was just about enough for me. I dried off and settled into the lounge chair.

The drive from Paris, the energetic workouts with Maddie, the glass of wine, swimming one length of the pool. It all suddenly seemed to work together and suggest I should maybe close my eyes for a minute or two and relax. I promptly fell asleep.

When I woke, I slowly opened my eyes. There were now four women sitting around the pool. Two directly across from me sipping what looked like Champagne, unfortunately, with their tops on. Off to my left were two other women. The fairly attractive woman was sitting on the edge of a lounge chair. She wore sandals, shorts, and a light-blue blouse. She was talking to her topless friend.

The friend was stretched out on a lounge chair with her eyes closed. Her massive body oozed over the sides of the chair, and her skin was so white you had to squint to look, not that I wanted to. I could see the red stretch marks from where I sat and guessed her weight as north of three hundred pounds.

I studied my stomach, the sun was bright, and it took a long moment of squinting before the pink registered. Bright pink. Suddenly, painful bright pink. I moved the elastic waist on the swimsuit a quarter of an inch. After sleeping in the unrelenting sun, a definite line appeared pink, heading toward scalding red, and then white, where the swimsuit had protected me just a moment before. Looking further down, my legs appeared to be candy apple red. During the process of sleeping, I seemed to have acquired one hell of a sunburn. I quickly sat up, felt the searing pain on my stomach and face. I wrapped the towel around my waist and hurried back into the locker room, where I stared at myself in the full-length mirror. "You idiot," I said to my reflection. My red face looked like I was about to suffer a heart attack. I dressed carefully and hurried out of the locker room.

"How did you enjoy your swim, sir?" The guy behind the counter asked. The woman next to him simply stared with wide eyes, suggesting she couldn't believe what she was seeing.

"I had a nice swim. A very nice swim," I said and hurried out the door and back to the Prestige Suite. I stood in front of the bathroom mirror. Against the gleaming white tiles, my skin looked scarlet with crisp lines exposing where the swim trunks had been. A couple of white wrinkle lines ran across my stomach. My ears felt like they were on fire, and my nose looked like the red light on the top of an ambulance. I was red enough to blend into the silk wallpaper. I heard the door to the suite open.

"Dev?" Maddie called.

"I'm in the bathroom," I said and gingerly wrapped a fluffy white bath towel around my waist before I stepped into the room.

Maddie was arranging a half dozen colored shopping bags on the end of the bed, shades of her shopping trip a few days ago in Paris. "Wait until you see what I . . . Oh, my God. Dev? What the hell happened to you? Are you okay? Oh, you poor thing."

"Hi, Maddie. I guess I sort of fell asleep for a couple of minutes and got a little sunburn."

"A little . . . Are you okay? You look positively fried. Does it hurt?"

"Umm, it's maybe not the most comfortable I've ever been."

"Oh, you poor thing. Did you put anything on that."

"Like what? Butter?"

"You had better get some cream on that. Let me run down to that little shop in the lobby. I'm sure they'll have something there that will reduce the pain and limit some of the damage. What were you thinking?"

"Thinking? It's not like I did this on purpose. I swam a bunch of laps," I lied, and then I closed my eyes for a couple of minutes, and this is what happened.

"A couple of minutes? I'm guessing more like a couple of hours, and in the sun. I don't suppose you put anything on like sun cream. Did you sit around and stare at topless women?"

"There weren't any. Oh wait, there was one, but she was more like the poster child for why there's a law against going topless at home."

"Let me run down and see if I can get some creams. You stay right there until I get back."

"Maddie, look at me. Where, exactly, do you think I'm going to go?"

Thirty-seven

Maddie told me two or three times what the name of the cream was, but I still couldn't remember. She slathered the stuff all over me, and I immediately began to feel better. Just now, I was lying in bed on two fluffy white towels while Maddie pulled various items out of the shopping bags to show me what she'd purchased. The shoes were black with red soles and heels, long, thin heels. "Christina Louboutin," she said proudly.

"Who's that? Did she wear them first?"

"Wear? No, dopey. She designed them. Aren't they just to die for?"

"Yeah, gorgeous."

"Okay, now check this out." She turned around, so her back was to me and pulled something out of a gold-colored shopping bag with writing in French all across the front. She turned around, grinning. She was holding up a short, very short, red sequined dress. She held it by the shoulder straps. It wasn't much longer than a t-shirt.

"Oh, wow, Maddie, I don't know."

"What's wrong? What don't you like?"

"Oh, no. I don't just like it. I love it. I'm worried if you wear that to dinner, there'll be so many guys lining up to talk to you that you won't have time for me."

"Oh, you are so sweet. Thank you. So you like it?"

"Like it?" I said. "I love it. I've always been into sequins."

"For your information, these aren't sequins, Dev. This is a double strap, red rhinestone wrap dress."

"Yeah, that's exactly what I thought it was."

"Yeah, right. Did you remember to make our dinner reservation?"

"Yes, I did. Eight o'clock, but I'm going to call back and tell them to make sure we're sitting at a table in a dark corner."

She rolled her eyes and looked at the clock on the fireplace mantel. "Mmm, almost six. If you made an eight o'clock reservation, I'd better get a move on. I'm going to grab a shower. I want you to lie there and just let that cream do its work. You'll feel a lot better in another hour."

Surprisingly, Maddie was right. The cream had soothed my sunburn substantially. I climbed out of bed at seven. Maddie was still in the bathroom. I knocked on the door.

"Come on in," she called. I stepped into the bathroom. Maddie was seated at a small makeup table in front of a three-sided mirror. She had another round mirror positioned in front of her that magnified her face. She was currently working on her eye makeup. Just like me, she had a fluffy white towel wrapped around her. Only she looked about a thousand times sexier in her towel.

"Feeling any better?" she asked, staring into the round mirror and not bothering to take a look at me. She set one brush down and picked up another.

"Definitely took a good deal of the pain away." I walked over and stood in front of the mirror above the vanity. "Now, if it could just do something with this color." The reflection staring back at me was scarlet. I looked like I was about to explode from high blood pressure.

"Oh, in about a week that will, hopefully, begin to fade," Maddie said. She was in the process of applying sparkly red eye shadow. She'd already done the black eyeliner that trailed off to a point beyond her eyes. She was in the midst of her two-hour makeup marathon.

"Wow, you look great, Maddie."

"Thanks. Umm, any idea what you're going to wear?"

"Yeah, whatever I have in my suitcase. I think I forgot to pack a tuxedo, so it'll just be black jeans and a sweater."

She closed her beautiful eyes for a long moment and took a couple of deep breaths to calm herself. "You didn't bring anything else?"

"I've packed some pretty cool t-shirts. I got a white one that says Saint Paul Saints. A green one that says Jingle Bells. A black one that—"

"Dev, you are not wearing a t-shirt to our dinner to-night. Would you happen to have a shirt with a collar and some buttons that you could wear with that sweater you have?"

"Yeah, I think so, maybe."

"Good. After you shower and shave, you can put them on. I'll be finished in here in a few minutes, and then the bathroom will be all yours."

"It was more like forty-five minutes, but what did I care. I cautiously shaved, and stepped into the shower for possibly the quickest shower of my life. The water felt like it was peeling the sunburned skin from my body. I lathered up and rinsed off in about two minutes. I reapplied the cream Maddie had gotten for me and carefully dressed. Because of my sunburned stomach, I decided not to wear a belt and just let the sweater cover that fact. I had a short sleeve Hawaiian print shirt, blue with pineapples all over it.

I took the shirt out of my suitcase and walked back into the bathroom. "This shirt okay for tonight?"

She had a look on her face suggesting she might get sick. "You are so not wearing that. No. Not allowed. Where did you get that thing, anyway?"

"My closet. I've got a bunch of them at home. I—"

"Somehow, I'm not surprised. Do you have another shirt?"

"Well, yeah but this—"

"Wear the other shirt and throw that monstrosity away. Please."

Thirty-eight

At one minute before eight, Maddie stepped into her double strap, red rhinestone wrap dress. It was worth waiting just watching her slink the thing up and over her hips. "Zip me up," she said once the double straps were on her shoulders.

I zipped the dress, pulling hard to get the zipper up the last two inches, afraid I might tear the thing. She let out an audible exhale once I stepped back.

"What do think?" she said, turning around in front of me.

She was beautiful. The dress almost didn't cover her perfect bum, and the subtle imprint of an extremely tiny thong was the icing on the cake. "The term drop-dead gorgeous doesn't do you justice. You'll be the hottest looking woman in the place, Maddie. Great choice on the dress."

"Thank you. Now bring me my shoes, will you?" She pointed to the shoebox in the corner.

I took the shoes out of the box, examining them as I did so. The insole was black with a squiggly signature. Below the signature, the word 'Paris' was in gold script. I set the shoes down in front of her. She placed her hands on my shoulders and then stepped into the shoes. She rose a good four inches.

"You going to be able to walk in those things?"

"I'll be fine. Just as long as you stay within reach."

We headed down to the dining room. As we walked through the lobby, the normally attentive front desk staff were all glued to a tv. It looked like they were watching some sort of local fire on the news. The dining room was full but quiet. Everyone was talking in muffled tones.

As the maître d' led us back to our table, we passed two couples where the women had tears running down their face. We passed a couple seated in front of a window. The guy had just heaped some sort of concoction on a piece of bread and was bringing it up to his mouth. He stopped with his mouth open, ready to take a bite, and moved his head following Maddie as she strutted past in a dress that couldn't possibly be any shorter. The woman at his table, presumably his wife, punched him in the shoulder. She said something in French that I obviously couldn't understand, but from the tone, her message was clear. He wouldn't be getting any action tonight.

The maître d' pulled out Maddie's chair, ran his eyes up and down her figure for a moment, and handed me my menu. "Enjoy your dinner. Your server will be here in just the moment." He didn't smile.

"Can I ask you what's going on? Everyone seems upset. The front desk was focused on a fire on the TV. Two women are crying at their tables. What's happened?"

"You have not heard?"

"Heard what?"

"In Paris. The Cathedral of Notre Dame. It is burning."

"Burning? We went past it a couple of days ago. They were doing all sorts of restoration work on it."

He nodded. "Yes, the restoration. And now, there is the fire." He suddenly looked like he was ready to cry and said, "Please, you must excuse me. Enjoy your meal." He turned and hurried away from our table.

"The cathedral? That big one we saw in Paris is burning?" Maddie said.

"Yeah, sounds like it."

We ordered dinner and ate mostly in silence. Everyone in the dining room appeared devastated. Two tables over a woman was sobbing uncontrollably, while her husband rubbed her shoulders. She finally brushed his hand away and hurried out of the room.

"This is getting to be a real downer," I said.

"Dev, that Cathedral must be really important to Paris," Maddie said.

"Yeah, but take a look around. Apparently, not just Paris. I think for all of France and maybe for the rest of the world as well."

The maître d' suddenly appeared with two glasses of wine. "Madame, monsieur. Please, my apology. This fire is so upsetting."

"Oh, really, that is very kind, but it's not necessary. We understand. The fire is so tragic."

"Please, I must insist," he said, setting the glasses down in front of us.

"Thank you. You are very kind," I said. We both raised our glasses, and I said, "To Notre Dame. And, to the rebuild."

Two guys at the table next to us sort of whipped their heads around. One held his glass up to us, and his pal stood with his glass and shouted, "Reconstruire."

Suddenly, everyone in the room began to stand repeating whatever that word meant. They were all toasting, raising their wine glasses.

"Oh, Jesus. What did you start, Dev? Are we in trouble?" Maddie said.

The last thing I remember is singing a Garth Brooks song with the maître d' and some other guy. Everyone in the restaurant was buying wine for everyone else. Maddie was seated in a way that pretty much left her completely exposed. She was fighting to keep her eyes open and her head up. God only knows how, but we somehow made it back to the Prestige Suite.

Thirty-nine

Maddie suddenly mumbled, "I need some aspirin. A lot of aspirin," I rolled over and attempted to focus on her. She was still wearing the red rhinestone wrap dress. Sort of. It was scrunched around her waist. The silk sheets on her side of the bed were covered in shiny little red objects. "Looks like maybe you weren't supposed to wear the dress to bed."

"Did you hear what I said?" She mumbled

"Okay. Okay. Let me see if there's any in the bathroom." I groaned as I stumbled out of bed and attempted to focus. I checked the drawers and the cabinet beneath the vanity. Empty. I stumbled back into the bedroom. The clock on the mantel read a quarter to eleven. "I'll have to go down and get some in the lobby. Be right back," I said and sat down on the edge of the bed.

Maddie was shaking me awake with her foot. I must have gone back to sleep for a brief moment. "Dev. Aspirin. Now." She groaned. Her eyes remained closed.

"I'm on it. Let me just get dressed." I pulled on my jeans and t-shirt, grabbed the keycard for the room, and left. There was a Champagne bottle in the hallway in front of our door. As I stepped out of the room, I knocked the bottle over, and it gurgled warm, flat liquid onto the hall carpet. I took my time on the stairs heading down to the lobby. I didn't realize I was barefoot until I stepped onto the cold tile floor in the shop. Fortunately, they had Bayer aspirin on the shelf. I grabbed the aspirin along with a couple of bottles of orange drink and headed back up to our room.

Maddie had a pillow piled on top of her head. I opened the aspirin bottle, shook out two, and unscrewed the cap off the orange drink bottle. "Maddie, here, roll over. I've got some aspirin for you."

She groaned and pulled a second pillow over her head. I took the two aspirin and chased them down with some orange drink. I set the aspirin bottle and the orange drink on the chest of drawers and climbed back into bed. I woke just before one in the afternoon. Maddie still had two pillows pulled over her head. I stared at her for a long moment to make sure she was still breathing. She was.

I rolled out of bed and went into the bathroom. I splashed warm water on my face and grimaced as a few drops of water landed on my sunburned chest. That pretty much ruled out a shower. I slowly got dressed. I debated waking Maddie, but couldn't land on a reason it would be worthwhile. So I quietly left the room. This time I was even wearing shoes and socks. I headed downstairs to the bistro restaurant and ordered a cheese-burger, fries, and coffee. I took my time eating. After about forty-five minutes, I went back up to our room.

Quietly, I opened the door. Maddie was out of bed. The aspirin bottle was open. The bottle of orange drink was empty, and next to it stood a can of something called Bridélice. The image on the can appeared to be whipped cream. The red rhinestone dress was on the floor just in front of the bathroom door. The door was closed, and I could hear the shower running. I decided privacy might be the best idea for the time being. I pulled the gold an-tique desk chair over in front of the window, settled in, and looked out the window as the world went by. Maddie stepped out of the bathroom a good half-hour later. She was wearing one of the white robes and carrying the other bottle of orange drink.

"How's the head?" I said.

"Improving. Slowly."

"You had some aspirin?"

"Yes. Thank you for getting that."

"You mind if I ask what's with the can of whipped cream?"

"You took it from the restaurant kitchen last night. I kicked it onto the floor when I rolled out of bed. You don't remember?"

"Maybe, sort of, I think."

She scoffed. "Well, you sure weren't complaining last night."

"You feel like getting some lunch?"

"I thought that's where you were, having lunch."

"I was, but you haven't eaten and—"

"And I think I might just take a pass and let my body recover from last night's craziness."

"Yeah, things definitely got a little crazy. When I was down in the lobby, I saw a newspaper. I think they're going to rebuild the cathedral or at least attempt it."

"Really. Oh, that would be great. Of course, it might take a year or two."

"Yeah, or fifty. You sure you don't want to grab some lunch?"

"You know," she seemed to think for a long moment. "Yeah, maybe we could take a walk. Look around in the town, and if we see a restaurant I like, we could stop there and grab something."

"Okay, you get dressed, and we'll go. You could wear your dress."

She slowly bent over and picked the dress up off the floor. "Unfortunately, I think last night might have been the first and last time I'll ever wear it. It wasn't really designed to be slept in."

"Yeah, I noticed a bunch of the sequins scattered around the bed."

"Yeah. Those were supposed to be rhinestones, but now I'm thinking they might just be rhinestone sequins. Some sort of special color or something." Maddie held the dress up by the shoulder straps. She shook it once or twice, and sparkly little sequins fluttered to the floor.

"God. One night and look at these spots where they've already worn off just from sitting and having dinner."

I could see no point in mentioning she slept in the dress, which also meant she was wearing it during our pre-sleep activity.

"Give me just a minute to throw something on, and we can go for a little walk. Okay?"

"Go ahead, take your time," I said since I knew she would anyway. While she was in the bathroom, I shoved the gun I took from those idiots outside of Pannier Champagne from my suitcase and shoved it in the back of my jeans. Careful to avoid my sunburn.

Forty

It was close to an hour rather than 'just a minute,' but we eventually strolled out of the hotel. We walked through the Parc de Champagne, a lovely little park, and onto a commercial street. Occasionally Maddie stopped and stared in the windows of a couple of clothing stores.

"You want to go in and look at something? I can just hang out here."

"Oh, thanks, but I was in there yesterday and didn't see anything I liked."

I wanted to ask, 'If that's the case, why are you stopping?' But what was the point? As we passed an Internet café, a guy was stepping out of the door. He was older, maybe late forties or fifty. He had a beard and bifocal glasses with thick lenses. As he saw us approaching, he stood in the doorway, smiled, and indicated we should enter with a gracious wave of his arm.

I smiled back and shook my head.

Maddie looked straight ahead and tried to ignore him.

He said something in French, not abusive sounding, but rather something sounding familiar like he knew us or at least knew Maddie. The only word I picked up was, "Mademoiselle." We kept on walking, and he called out again, this time leading with, "Mademoiselle Maddie." With the accent and a couple of other words, I was unable to tell if he may have even called her by name. Maddie seemed to pick up speed.

"Sounded like he knew you," I said, as I hurried to catch up.

"Or maybe wanted to. I get guys yelling stuff at me all the time. After a while, you learn to ignore it."

"Yeah, I get the same thing from women, too. Yelling at me. But they never sound all that friendly when they're doing it."

"Maybe you need a better figure," she said and smiled.

"Among other things."

We found a little bistro place that looked quiet and had a nice menu in English posted on the front window. Among other things, the menu featured breakfast all day long. "This looks perfect. You want to try it?" Maddie asked.

"As long as you're happy. I ate a while ago. I'm gonna just be grabbing a coffee."

We went in and sat in a booth. Maddie ordered scrambled eggs, sausages, toast, and tea. I ordered a coffee, and since they had them, a chocolate croissant. Once the food came, Maddie took a couple of bites then pushed the eggs and sausages around the plate.

"What? You don't like your breakfast?"

"Oh, no. It's good, very good. I feel like I've sort of had enough."

"You barely touched it."

"Oh, okay, dad. Back off."

"All right, not trying to cause any problems. But, if you're not going to finish it pass that plate over here."

"I thought you already ate?" Maddie said.

"I did, but that was almost two hours ago, and I figure a little snack wouldn't hurt. You know, just enough to hold me until dinner time."

She shook her head and passed the plate over to me. I dug in, and in a couple of minutes, I was cutting the last breakfast sausage in half and stuffing a piece into my mouth.

"You know what really gets me mad?" Maddie said.

"I thought you said you weren't going to finish this. If you wanted more, why did you pass your plate over to me?"

"No, not that. Eat up. It's fine. I mean, I get it, and I don't have a problem with that. But, what gets me mad is you won't put on so much as an ounce of weight after eating all that. All I have to do is look at the plate, and I'll probably gain a couple of pounds. It's so not fair."

"Maybe, but then again, I could probably walk into just about any bar, anywhere in the world, and no one is even going to give me a second look, let alone send a drink over and hope I'll smile and talk to them."

"Yeah, I guess there is that."

"Exactly. That guy on the way over who stepped out of that internet joint. Obviously, he was saying nice things, whatever they were. If it had just been me walking by, he wouldn't have looked twice unless he was checking out my sunburn. Or, he maybe would have thought I was in his way or something. But you walk by, and he wants to ask you out on a date."

"He might have been a little too old."

"And he might have been a millionaire too."

"Mmm, I didn't think of that. Might be a good idea to go back there. You ready to leave?"

"Just a minute," I said, then stabbed the last piece of sausage and shoved it into my mouth. "Okay, let's go." I paid the bill. As we stepped out the door, I took a right and headed back the way we came.

"Oh, let's take a different route back. See a couple of other streets. It's all so nice. I love just looking around. Maybe we could stop someplace and have a little glass of wine. What are we going to do back in the hotel, anyway."

" A glass of wine? Okay, your recovery must be working. Fine with me. You see a place you feel like going into, just say so. You're right. It's not like we're scheduled for anything later on tonight."

Maddie linked arms with me, gave me a peck on the cheek, and we headed in the opposite direction. We got lost on some streets. We were both used to our hometown where most of the streets run perpendicular. Not that it was a problem. There was plenty to see. After about forty minutes, we stopped in front of a little place with a long bar and a couple of tables. A couple was getting up from one of the tables.

"Let's check this place out," Maddie said.

Forty-one

We sat at the table the couple had left. Maddie ordered a glass of wine. I had a beer. Just sitting and chatting seemed to awaken Maddie's appetite, and we ordered a tray of different cheeses and some bread. We talked for another half hour about everything and nothing. It was turning to dusk when we stepped outside and began to make our way back to the hotel. We were standing on a corner with three other people waiting for the light to change. I was about to step off the curb when a horn honked, and a car raced through the intersection. The car was a Range Rover. A flat black Range Rover.

I thought I might have recognized the guy sitting in the front passenger seat. His nose was taped and covered with a green splint. Both eyes were black and appeared slightly swollen. There was something familiar with him. The Range Rover sped through the intersection on a yellow light. Obviously, trying to make it through before the light turned red. The man standing next to me muttered something in French. Whatever he said didn't sound all that complimentary.

I watched as the taillights faded into the distance. I noticed the Range Rover appeared to be leaning decidedly to the left. I immediately thought of the fat guy from the plane, Ali Debauche. The same guy who raced up the street as we fled that first hotel in Paris. The same guy who was waiting for us with his two thugs outside Pannier Champagne back in Château-Thierry.

It suddenly dawned on me. The nose in a splint and two black eyes was the guy who's head I slammed in the car door. They were driving a flat black Range Rover. How in the hell did they end up here? Maddie didn't have a phone. Did they get a call about the car we left at the train depot? I should have driven the damn thing into the river.

"Hello, anyone home? Are you coming? Or are you going to wait for the light to change again?" Maddie yelled. She was halfway across the street, and she'd turned to yell at me. "Come on, Dev. I don't want to wait for another five minutes until the light changes."

I stepped off the curb and caught up to her.

"Where'd you go? For a moment there, you looked like you were about a thousand miles away."

"Oh, you know. For a moment, I guess I was lost in my own little world."

She glanced over at me and rolled her eyes. "What do you feel like doing tonight?"

"Truthfully. If we simply hung around the hotel, it would be all right with me. I could be talked into taking a sauna when we get back. Get the final bit of impurities from last night's fun out of my system."

"No complaints from me if we went to bed early. At least earlier than last night."

"I can't be sure, but I think we were in bed around three," I said.

"Yeah, but Dev, we didn't go to sleep until about five."

"You're not going to hear any complaints from me."

We walked for another twenty minutes. I more or less followed Maddie, who seemed to know where she was going. Sure enough, about the time I was ready to ask if we needed to get directions, she turned, and there was our hotel on the far side of the park.

"Nice job of getting us here," I said.

"What? Did you think we were lost?"

"No, nothing like that. But I'm ready to sit in the sauna for a bit. Maybe, get cleaned up and have a leisurely evening nibbling on tasty things and sipping a beer."

"It might be more of the bubbly for me. After all, this is supposed to be the Champagne capital of France, isn't it?"

"Yeah, that's right, and that sounds like you're in the recovery mode. You have something appropriate to wear in the sauna?"

"Why don't we go down to the exercise area and see if anyone else is even there? It's the evening, and somehow, I'm thinking most folks will be getting ready for dinner and a night out on the town."

"Is that what you'd like to do?"

"A night on the town? Oh, no. Really, a sauna and a laid back night sounds like heaven to me right now. Believe me, I don't need any more excitement for a while," Maddie said.

"Sounds like an excellent plan." As we approached the hotel, I scanned the parking area for a flat black Range Rover. Fortunately, I didn't see one. Maybe I'd jumped to a hasty conclusion back on that busy corner. Maybe that Range Rover had broken shocks, and the guy with the nose splint was recovering from surgery. Yeah, maybe.

Forty-two

We walked down to the pool and exercise area with towels wrapped around us. I had my swimsuit on underneath. By all appearances, other than staff, we were the only ones in the place. The couple working behind the service counter smiled and wrote down our room number on a sheet. We each grabbed extra towels and walked through our appropriate locker rooms. Both locker rooms were completely empty. We met in the pool area. We were the only people there.

"How do a few minutes in the jacuzzi sound?"

"Like heaven," Maddie said.

I set the timer on the jacuzzi for twenty minutes, and we hopped in. I should rephrase that. Maddie hopped in. I gingerly inserted myself a quarter of an inch at a time, flinching as the latest section of my sunburned skin entered the water."

Maddie was sitting in the jacuzzi with water up almost to her chin. Three jacuzzi jets were now directed at her. "Oh. My. God. You are such a big baby, Dev. Just jump in and get it over with."

I gave a little whine as I stepped in, and the water rose above my knees. "I'm working my way in, slowly," I said. I was standing on the third of four steps into the jacuzzi. The water was now almost up to my waist. With my sunburn, it felt like a belt sander was running over my legs.

Maddie suddenly stood up. She was naked, and my immediate reflex was to focus on her breasts right at the waterline. She took a step toward me and ran her tongue over her lips. I looked around to make sure no one else was in the area thinking, *'this could get interesting.'* She suddenly grabbed my wrists and pulled me off my feet. I went under for a second or two.

"Ahh-ahh," I screamed for a long moment once I regained my footing and rose to the surface. I gradually calmed down as the pain began to subside. After a very long moment, I carefully took a seat and directed the water jets away from me.

"There, now that wasn't so bad, was it?"

"No, except for the near heart attack you almost gave me, it wasn't bad at all."

By the time our twenty minutes were up, and the water jets stopped, we were both ready to get out of the jacuzzi. Maddie wrapped a towel around her while I tossed mine over my shoulder. We headed into the sauna, climbed up to the top bench, and leaned back against the cedar wood walls. I immediately jerked forward, away from the scalding wall. Slowly, I settled back until I was reasonably comfortable, or at least as comfortable as one can get given the heat. We didn't talk much. In fact, we only said a couple of words and then concentrated on our breathing and basic survival. Once in a while, I ran my towel over my face. There was a water bucket with a wooden dipper so you could pour water over the heated rocks. I left it untouched, and fortunately, Maddie did the same. We forced ourselves to stay in the sauna for a total of sixteen minutes.

I made the first move to leave, saying, "I'll wait for you outside."

"It's no fun in here alone. I'm right behind you," Maddie said.

We hurried through the hotel lobby and up the stairs to our room. As I opened the door to our room, the couple in the suite next to us stepped into the hall. They both smiled and said, "Bonsoir."

We nodded, said the same to them. We hurried into our room and closed the door behind us. "Let me grab the first shower. I'll make it quick," Maddie said.

I stood at the foot of the bed with the damp towel wrapped around me and slowly grew colder. Much colder. Based on the clock on the mantel, Maddie had been in the shower for close to a half-hour. I was about to knock on the door when I heard the water turn off. A moment later, she stepped out of the bathroom with a towel wrapped around her. She was drying her hair with a second towel.

"You finally finished in there?" I said, so cold I had trouble getting the words out.

"For the moment," she said. "What's wrong with you? Are you shivering?"

"No. I'm dying from exposure after standing out here in a wet swimsuit while you took your time in the shower."

"Oh, God. Whatever. I don't suppose it ever dawned on you to take the swimsuit off. Well, go ahead. If you're so cold, get in the shower."

An hour later, we were receiving a half-dozen smiling nods from people in the dining room as we made our way to a table in the back. Maddie was dressed in another revealing little outfit. At least tonight, no one was punched by their wife as Maddie strutted past. We exchanged pleasantries with our new friend, the maître d', and ordered a couple of hors d'oeuvres. Maddie had a glass of wine. I had a beer. We shared a Crème Brûlée for dessert. This meant I had a spoonful, and Maddie had the rest. I made up for it with a second beer. We were in our room and in bed a little after ten. It was apparent nothing was going to happen, so I drifted off to sleep.

It was just after midnight when I woke. I had been dreaming about the Range Rover I'd seen earlier. The guy with the nose splint in the front seat, the car leaning to the left as it shot through the intersection up the slight rise and disappeared. Who was I kidding? It had to be that fat guy from the plane and his thug pals.

Maddie was sound asleep, breathing heavily. I was sitting in the gold chair with the red silk upholstery, staring out the window into the park. With the exception of the occasional car passing along the road at the far end of the park, there was no activity. The lights appeared to be dimmed around the hotel. The few hotel windows I could see were all darkened. All I heard was Maddie breathing and the clock on the mantel ticking.

Suddenly, there was a noise from out in the hall. Just a click. I listened and heard it again. It seemed to be coming from the door to our room. I hurried over to my side of the bed and grabbed the pistol resting on the nightstand. I cautiously tiptoed toward the entrance while aiming the gun at the door, just in case.

There it was again. This time two clicks. Someone was trying our doorknob. Fortunately, it was locked. A thin sliver of light seeped from the hallway beneath the bottom of the door. Two brief shadows appeared. Someone's feet? Another click on the doorknob, followed by a muffled voice. Only a word or two. Then nothing. There wasn't a peephole in the door, so I couldn't look out into the hall. I waited for what felt like an hour. I could feel my heart pounding and could only hope whoever it was didn't hear it out in the hall. I stared at the sliver of light beneath the door but couldn't detect any movement in the hall.

I held the pistol close to my chest. I carefully opened the door and stepped into the hallway. It was empty. I thought I might have heard the elevator door close, but I wasn't sure. There had definitely been someone out in the hall attempting to turn the doorknob. I examined the door frame opposite the knob. The scratches appeared to be recent, and I noted small flakes of paint on the hall-way carpet. I stepped back inside and quietly closed the door to the room. I triple checked the lock. I wedged the gold desk chair beneath the doorknob and climbed back into bed. I never did fall back asleep.

Forty-three

I t was after ten the following morning before Maddie finally woke up. The only reason she was even awake was because I'd finally figured out how to turn the TV on using the remote. I was currently watching some cartoon starring a little duck that wasn't all that funny. I kept pretending I was asleep and rolled onto Maddie. She pushed me off but never seemed to wake. I closed my eyes and let my hand drop onto her shoulder as if I'd been asleep, hoping she'd wake up. Nothing worked. Based on the way she eventually woke up after sleeping for the better part of twelve hours, she didn't seem to be buying any of my attempts.

"God, what is wrong with you? No, we're not going to have sex if that's what you were planning on. I'm finally able to sleep in for the first time this week, and you go ahead and ruin it. And what dreadful thing are you watching, anyway?"

"I don't know what this is. I was asleep, and this trash came on," I lied. "I thought you were watching tv, so I didn't say anything. Besides, you woke me up."

"Yeah, sure I did. So where's the remote?"

"I thought you had it."

"Where's the remote, Dev." She suddenly sounded very serious.

"How the hell should I know. It's gotta be around here somewhere. I just . . ."

"Nice try. Give it to me. It's right there on your end table."

"What? Oh yeah, sure enough. Gee, I didn't—"

"Shut up and give me the damn thing," she said. She rolled over on top of me and grabbed the remote. I thought there might be a chance, but just as quickly, she rolled off. "You can be such a jerk sometimes," she said. She pressed a button on the remote, and the TV suddenly went blank. For a moment, it was painfully quiet in the room. "Okay, I'm going back to sleep. I do not want to be disturbed. If you get bored, you can take a shower, get dressed, and go downstairs and have breakfast. I will not be joining. Clear?"

You sure you don't want to—"

"What part of no, don't you understand? 'N' 'O' spells no. Now, I do not wish to be bothered in any way, shape, or form. So you, get your ass out of this bed. I'm going back to sleep."

I looked at her for a long moment trying to decide if there was an outside chance I could remain.

She took my pillow and shoved it between us. She pulled another pillow over her head, and from beneath it said, "Did you hear what I said, Dev? Get your butt out of this bed. I'm not kidding."

I quickly hopped out of bed and stood looking at her.

After a long moment, she peeked out from beneath the pillow. Her eyes flared, and she said, "God. You can be so stupid sometimes. Now good night." With that, she rolled over on her side, facing the wall. She pulled the duvet cover up and over her head just in case I hadn't gotten the message.

I stood there for another minute or two, hoping maybe there was a chance. I finally grabbed my clothes, tiptoed into the bathroom, and closed the door. I shaved, took a quick shower, and dressed. I slowly opened the bathroom door and tiptoed out of the bathroom. I picked up my shoes and a keycard and headed for the door. Maddie was breathing deeply, almost snoring. I let myself out into the hall, closed the door as quietly as possible, and made my way downstairs to breakfast.

I'd finished breakfast and was on my third cup of coffee when Maddie strolled into the restaurant. The extra hour and a half of sleep seemed to have worked wonders. She was actually smiling. She kissed me on the forehead before she sat down and said, "Oh, thanks for letting me sleep. I feel so much better."

"Yeah, you seemed really tired. I thought it might be best if I quietly left the room," I said. There was no benefit to be gained going over her tirade. We chatted while she had a bowl of fruit with some granola for breakfast and two cups of coffee.

When she was finally finished, she pushed the bowl away and said, "What do you feel like doing today?"

"I feel like heading for Amsterdam and getting on a flight and going back to the states."

"Now? You don't want to check things out? Have a little fun?"

"I'm thinking we're pressing our luck, and we've been on borrowed time ever since we landed in Paris. Those guys haven't stopped looking for us. Would you if someone took that money from you? I don't know what sort of resources they have. But why wait to find out? They aren't going to be fooling around. If they find us, they're not going to be interested in cutting us any sort of break, so let's get back to the states and deal with the devil we know, namely Tubby Gustafson. He's liable to welcome you with open arms when you bring that money to him. Besides, he can provide protection."

"But Amsterdam? My return ticket has me flying out of Paris."

"Don't you think they might know that?"

"I don't know. I was thinking—"

"Maddie, if they know you were on the same flight as that fat guy flying over, I'd say there's a pretty good chance they know when you're scheduled to fly back. Don't forget, they most likely read the itinerary in your suitcase. And even if they didn't, it wouldn't take much to stick a couple of guys in the Paris airport to wait for you on the odd chance you decide to show up."

"Yeah, maybe," she said and seemed to think about that.

"Look, Maddie. Sooner or later we're going to have to go back. It just seems to me, if we do it now rather than later, we're in a much better position to tell Tubby we have almost all of the money for him even though the odds are stacked against us. We know someone was shot at that first hotel. We know they were, somehow, able to follow us to Château-Thierry and probably would have jumped us if you hadn't changed your hair and disappeared out the door with that group of students. I think we're already on borrowed time here in Reims." I didn't want to upset her by telling her I thought someone was at the door of our suite in the middle of last night.

"So, Amsterdam?"

"Yes, major international airport. They'll probably have flights leaving for the US all day long. We don't have to fly to the Twin Cities. In fact, it would probably be a good idea to fly to New York, DC, Boston, or maybe even Atlanta and take a flight from there into the twin cities."

"How are we supposed to get from here to Amsterdam?"

"I've already checked that out. All we have to do is take the train. I talked to the woman out at the front desk. The trip takes four to six hours, depending. The first train left at six forty-five this morning. The last one leaves at nine-fifteen tonight and gets to Amsterdam around three in the morning. Once we get to Amsterdam, we can buy two first-class tickets back to the states on whatever flight has space available."

"You really think we need to do this?"

"Yeah, Maddie, I do. The longer we're over here, the riskier it's going to get. I have no doubt these guys already know we're somewhere in this city or, if they don't, they soon will."

"But how?"

"I don't know, and I don't want to find out."

She seemed to think for another long moment. "How about this? Let me do a little more shopping around today. We grab that late train to Amsterdam tonight. What time did you say it leaves here, nine-fifteen?"

"Actually, nine-twelve, but yeah."

"Okay, let me have an afternoon of shopping. We grab a quiet dinner. Hop on that train, and we arrive in Amsterdam just after three in the morning. We take a taxi to the airport, get our tickets, and clear security before the sun is up."

I had to admit, in a weird way, that sort of made some sense. Who would be at the Amsterdam train station in the middle of the night? "Okay, tell you what. You give me your keycard to the room."

"What?"

"I'll wait up there with our luggage, and whenever you get back, we'll head to the train station."

"You don't trust me."

"Let's just say I've had to deal with Tubby Gustafson over the years, and I don't trust him. This way, we'll both be safe."

"That's a good idea because, when I give you my keycard, you can give me your passport."

"My passport?"

"I can't get in the room without the keycard. You can't get on a plane without your passport. See?"

Forty-four

I waited in the room for Maddie to return. I sat in the gold chair with the red silk upholstery and stared out the window, searching for any sign of a flat black Range Rover. Fortunately, I never saw one. When I wasn't staring out the window, I continually checked to see that the metal briefcase was still behind the drapes. A little after five, a taxi pulled up, and Maddie slid out of the back seat. The taxi driver climbed out, stepped to the rear of the vehicle, and opened the trunk. He reached in and handed Maddie a half dozen different shopping bags. They smiled and nodded at one another. Maddie, with bags in hand, headed for the hotel door while he stood and stared, taking in the view for a very long moment as she strutted towards the front entrance.

She knocked on the door a few minutes later. When I opened it, she hurried into the suite and dumped the various shopping bags on the bed.

"Oh, what a day," she said. She sat on the end of the bed, kicked off her shoes, leaned back, and closed her eyes. "I'm beat."

"Yeah, I suppose shopping for five or six hours will do that to you. Did you find anything you liked?" I said, eyeing the half dozen shopping bags scattered across the bed.

"Oh, a couple of things. Hey, if we're going to catch that train tonight, I had better hit the shower. How about we grab something to eat at a bistro or one of those little restaurants we walked past yesterday. I don't feel like doing the fancy dining room downstairs. That okay with you?"

"Yeah, go ahead and grab your shower. If we're going to eat somewhere, we should probably be out of here in the next hour or so. Even if we're in some laid back place, it's going to take an hour to eat dinner, and we'll still have to get to the train station and buy our tickets."

"Calm down, Dev. We've got plenty of time. I'm going to grab a quick shower, and maybe we can find a McDonald's or something. You know, so we can eat really fast and save time. That way, we can get our train tickets and still be able to sit on our ass waiting in the train station for two damn hours."

"Very funny."

She pulled a grey, short sleeve sweater from one of the shopping bags, a pair of black slacks from another, and arranged them on the bed. She grabbed her makeup bag and headed into the bathroom. She closed the door, and a second later, I heard the lock snap. I stuck the pistol into the back of my jeans and pulled my shirt out to cover it. I took the briefcase from behind the drapes and returned it to her suitcase. Forty minutes later, I heard the shower turn off. A half-hour after that, the bathroom door opened, and she stepped out.

"There. Now was that so bad?"

"No. You were right. A quick shower and you look like a million bucks. Well worth the wait." She appeared oblivious to my comment.

"Let me just get dressed, and we can get out of here."

Amazing the amount of time it can take to pull on a pair of slacks and a short-sleeved sweater. After another forty minutes of going back and forth from the bathroom to the bed, she said, "Okay, just about finished. Let me just pack my suitcase and—"

"Tell you what. Your quick shower and just getting dressed took the better part of two hours. We need to check out, grab a taxi, and get to the train station. Maybe, I should pack your suitcase."

She moved her head up and down, examining me. "That's what you're wearing? You're not going to get cleaned up or change?"

"Maddie. I'm a guy. We're going to be sitting on a train for a number of hours. Believe me. Absolutely no one cares what I wear, and that includes me. I could wear this shirt and jeans for the next week, and no one would even notice."

"I'd notice. In fact, I've noticed you've worn that shirt and jeans for the last four or five days."

"Maybe, but you're always mad at me anyway. So, what difference does it make?"

She flashed a look like she wanted to kill me. She opened her suitcase, crammed the shopping bags and her makeup bag around the metal briefcase, and zipped the suitcase closed. "There. Fast enough for you, Mister Hyper?"

"Yeah, perfect. Let's get out of here."

She reached in her pocket and thrust my passport at me in a stabbing sort of motion. We both did a quick check of the room, looking for anything we might have left behind. I checked the bathroom and found a mascara tube and lipstick.

"You left these," I said and held them out to her. She snatched them from me. I opened her suitcase, flicked the locks on the metal briefcase, and took a bundle of money out.

"What do you think you're doing?"

"I want to see if they'll exchange these dollars for euros. I can pay for the room and have enough cash to get the train tickets and pay for our flights."

She shook her head, draped her new purse over her shoulder and headed out the door. I stacked my suitcase on top of hers and hurried down the hall to catch up. She was stepping onto the elevator when I finally caught up.

The hotel charged us for the night, not that I cared. It wasn't my money. They exchanged my dollars for euros at some incredibly exorbitant rate. When we stepped outside, a taxi was just in the process of dropping off a well-dressed couple, and we were able to grab the cab. I tossed our luggage into the trunk, and we headed to the train station. I purchased two first-class tickets to Amsterdam. On the way to wheeling our luggage down to the train platform, I bought a bratwurst and a candy bar. "You want anything, Maddie."

She didn't bother to respond and instead kept walking towards the platform. I took a few minutes to eat the bratwurst, unwrapped the candy bar, and followed.

Forty-five

At this hour, the Reims train station was relatively quiet. No one had been ahead of us in line to purchase tickets. I was the only person ordering a bratwurst. Although, after tasting it, I had a pretty good idea of why that might be. I only passed three other people before I caught up with Maddie heading to the platform. We waited for about ten minutes before the train arrived. All the while, we were the only people standing on the platform.

As the train arrived, a conductor stepped off the train and onto the platform. He looked at our tickets and directed us to our cabin. The cabin seated six, but since we were the only ones in it, we promptly spread out across the seats. The conductor stepped into our cabin about ten minutes after we left the station and punched our tickets. Over the next hour, Maddie seemed focused on something else and responded in one-word answers to my attempts at starting a conversation. Eventually, we both drifted off to sleep.

If we'd stopped anywhere along the way to Amsterdam, I slept through it. There was a knock on the door to our cabin, someone half yelled something and opened the door. I sat up and was about to reach for the gun tucked in my belt when I realized it was the conductor. "Amsterdam. Fifteen minutes," he said and closed the door.

Maddie was stretched out on the seats across from me, lightly snoring. I reached over and gently shook her shoulder. "Maddie. Maddie, we're coming into Amsterdam. It's time to wake up."

"What? We're there already?"

"Yeah, we'll be in the train station in about fifteen minutes. You okay?"

"I guess. Wow, I was really out. Fifteen minutes?"

"Yeah," I said and slipped into my shoes. I stood, stretched, and looked out the windows. We were slowing down and passing through some sort of industrial area with a lot of one and two-story structures. Large dumpsters stood alongside old buildings, and tall fences with what looked like razor wire strung along the top surrounded the structures.

"Hey, Dev, sorry I was so bitchy earlier. I'm, I don't know, worried about the flight on the one hand and kinda wishing we could stay. I'm not looking forward to having to deal with Tubby Gustafson when we get back home."

"Don't worry about it, Maddie. Once he sees that you've got the funds, all your troubles will be over. Might be nice sometime to come back here and enjoy the experience, actually. You know, without having to be looking over our shoulder, constantly."

"Yeah, well, don't take this the wrong way, but I'd maybe think about coming back on my own. I keep thinking about what we talked about a couple of days ago. You know, about teaching kids English."

"Oh, yeah, you said you always wanted to be a teacher. You finish up that college stuff, and you could do that. You'd be good at it, Maddie."

"Thanks. I know one thing for sure. I'm done dancing for tips at the Centerfold Cabaret, or anywhere else for that matter. I feel like I've got an opportunity to do whatever I want, and you know what?"

"What?"

"I'm going to grab that opportunity. From now on, I'm going to be in charge of my own destiny."

"Good for you, Maddie. I think that's a great idea. Some people either never get the chance, or they never take the chance to do that. Jump in with both feet. Does that mean you're going to go to college?"

"Mmm, maybe. I'm not exactly sure, but I do know I'm not going to go back to what I was doing. What's the old saying? Strike while the iron's hot?"

"Yeah, or maybe, there's no time like the present. Anyway, good for you, Maddie."

She nodded slowly and repeated, "Yeah, Dev. There's no time like the present."

The train was suddenly pulling into the station. We gradually slowed along an empty platform and finally stopped. I couldn't see anyone anywhere, but then again, it was after three in the morning. Maddie got up and stretched once the train came to a stop. I opened the cabin door for Maddie and grabbed hold of the suitcases.

"Thanks, Dev. You know, sometimes, you're kind of okay." She reached up, gave me a peck on the cheek, and headed out the door. We were part of maybe only a dozen people climbing off the train. Two couples ahead of us had obviously been partying for a fair amount of time and were feeling no pain as they staggered toward the entrance to the station. Maddie kept looking around like she was searching for something. She stopped, stretched, and said, "You want me to take my suitcase?"

"No, don't worry about it."

"You sure? I'm a big girl. I can deal with it."

"Relax, I got 'em."

We walked along the platform toward the entrance to the station. Maddie stopped at a vending machine next to the entrance to the station and started to dig in her purse.

"Maddie, if you're hungry, we can get something once we get to the airport. We'll grab a taxi outside, and it shouldn't take longer than thirty or forty minutes to get there."

"Calm down. We've got hours to get there. I'm going to grab a candy bar. I might even share some with you if you're nice. God only knows you could use some sweetening. You know, we've been here for the better part of a week, and I still can't tell the difference between these euro coins. And two euros for a candy bar? You gotta be kidding me."

"You need some change?"

"No, thanks. I've got it in here, somewhere."

She continued to rummage around in her purse. I glanced up and down the platform. Other than the conductor and two other people in uniform heading toward us, we were now the only people on the platform. As they approached, the conductor smiled and said, "Have a pleasant evening." They all nodded, walked past us and into the entrance to the station.

"Ah, here we go. Hey, look at this, a two-euro coin. Perfect." Maddie said and held the coin up to me. She put the coin into the candy machine and pressed a button. A moment later, the candy bar dropped down, and she grabbed it.

"Great. Now, can we get out of here?"

"You're such a crab. What's the rush? We've got—"

"How nice of you to wait for us," a voice said. We turned and stared. His nose was still in a splint, but the swelling around his eyes had disappeared. What used to be two black eyes were now more of a faded brownish color on the outer edges of his cheekbones. And then there was the gun he pointed at us.

Forty-six

He pointed the pistol at me. "Don't even think about trying to act like a hero, Monsieur," The nose splint made his voice sound as if he had a severe cold. He waved his gun, indicating we should step back. "And the hands, get them up, up, up, the both of you."

His short, stocky friend, the guy with the two eyebrows above his left eye, suddenly appeared behind him and said, "Where is it? The briefcase belonging to Monsieur Debauche."

"I don't know what you're—"

Two eyebrows stepped forward and slapped me twice. "Stop with the lies. Where is it? Tell me now, or else."

I indicated Maddie's suitcase with a nod of my head.

He grabbed my suitcase from on top of Maddie's and tossed it across the platform toward the train. He wheeled Maddie's suitcase a few feet away, muttered something in French as he sneered at us, and kicked the suitcase onto the ground.

The fat guy suddenly appeared, out of breath and red-faced. He stood and gasped for a long moment or two in an effort to catch his breath. He said something, and Two Eyebrows knelt down, unzipped Maddie's suitcase, and pulled it open. The metal briefcase was just as Maddie had packed it, roughly in the middle with a half dozen shopping bags filled with designer clothes wedged around it. Fatty made another comment in French, and Two Eyebrows flipped the locks on the briefcase. He shot a look at Fatty, rubbed his hands together, counted to three, and lifted the lid on the metal briefcase. There it was looking back at him, just waiting to be picked up and caressed. The better part of a million bucks, of course, minus our hotels, meals, and Maddie's shopping sprees.

All three of them giggled. Two Eyebrows made the OK sign with his thumb and index finger, kissed his hand, and slammed the lid closed. He clicked both locks in place, slowly stood with an evil grin on his face, and stepped toward Maddie. He pulled a long black zip tie from his pocket, grabbed Maddie by the wrists, and pulled her arms behind her.

Based on the sound, I thought the jerk with the gun had spit, but then his eyes rolled into his head. He took a half step forward and dropped to the ground. He lay there, face down, as the Merda brothers suddenly appeared. Big Tony held a gun with a silencer attached to the barrel. Lurch stood behind him. As I pulled my pistol out, Two Eyebrows jumped at me. He grabbed for my gun, and it went off, knocking him backward. He gave me a sort of blank look before he crumpled to the ground.

Big Tony pulled Maddie in front of him and placed the gun to her head. "Drop the gun, Haskell, or she gets it. Don't even think about it," he said as I sized up the chances of shooting him. "Even if you shot me, I'll still squeeze the trigger. Either way, she'll be dead."

"Don't, Dev. Please, don't shoot. I don't want to die."

Big Tony watched me. When I lowered my gun, he said, "Put it on the ground and kick it over here."

I placed the pistol on the ground and kicked it across the platform to him.

"Good, now, lay face down with your hands stretched out."

I gave him a look, but then stretched out on the platform. As soon as I was down, Lurch was on top of me with his knee in the small of my back.

Fatty slowly backed up, turned, and attempted to escape. He was waddling toward the far end of the platform. Big Tony took two steps, aimed carefully, and put four rounds into him from a distance of about fifteen feet. Fatty jerked and stumbled as each round found its mark. He staggered up against one of the train cars and slid down the side, wedging his body between the train car and the edge of the platform. Everyone stared for a long moment, and he remained perfectly still.

"It's about damn time," Maddie said. "I don't think they had the best of intentions for me. What the hell took you so long?" She bent down and picked my pistol up from the platform.

"You kidding?" Big Tony said. "The streets are all curvy, and none of the signs are in English. You're lucky we made it here at all."

"Yeah, and not a moment too soon. How'd these jerks even know we were here?" Maddie said.

"I'm guessing they hacked your email account like they did your phone. When you emailed us yesterday afternoon, they must have gotten the information."

"Maddie?" I said, and Lurch applied more pressure to the small of my back with his knee.

She ignored me and looked at the three bodies on the platform. A pool of blood was slowly spreading around the guy with the nose splint. Two eyebrows sported a hole about the size of a dime in the middle of his forehead. His eyes had a very distant, glazed look. A small bit of blood ran down to the bridge of his nose. "We need to get out of here, like now," Maddie said, taking hold of the briefcase.

"What do you want us to do with your main squeeze here?" Lurch said.

Maddie glanced around and focused on a bench next to the vending machine. "Tie him to that bench. Use the plastic thingy that idiot was going to put on me. Check that guy's pockets. He's probably got some more of those."

"Why don't we just shoot him?"

"Because Tubby will deal with him once he goes back to the states. We shoot him, and Tubby'll know we did it. We leave him here, by the time the cops let him go, we'll all be long gone and back in the states.

"Wouldn't it be better if we—"

"No, it wouldn't, so quit arguing. Tie him up, and let's get going."

"Okay, okay. Lurch, you heard the lady."

Lurch picked up the twist tie from the platform and grabbed me by my arm. He pushed me over to the bench on the far side of the candy machine. He wrapped the zip tie around my wrist and pulled it tight, securing me to the steel arm on the bench. Big Tony rummaged through Two Eyebrows pockets and pulled out more zip ties.

"All right, we ready?" Maddie said after a few minutes.

Lurch tightened the final zip tie around my wrist. "Good to go," he said.

"Then let's get out of here before someone wanders down and sees us." She picked up the briefcase and said to Lurch, "You grab my suitcase." Lurch grabbed her suitcase. He and Big Tony stepped into the hallway that led to the terminal. Maddie stopped for a moment and looked at me. She seemed to be thinking. She shook her head, suddenly stepped over, and kissed me on the cheek.

"Maddie, what the hell are you doing? What's going on? You emailed these guys from that Internet café, didn't you?"

"Like you said, Dev. No time like the present. Give Tubby my best. *See ya*," she said and hurried off the platform.

My arms were strung out and zip-tied to the steel bench. I struggled to get loose but to no avail. "Maddie?" I called. "Maddie, don't leave me here. Maddie?"

I heard her distant voice calling Big Tony a few seconds later. A moment or two after that, three shots rang out, echoing across the platforms. Suddenly all was quiet.

"Maddie? Maddie?"

I pulled and strained against the zip ties until my arms hurt. Maybe twenty minutes later, I heard a scream out in the hallway. A few minutes after that, two police officers entered the platform. They were dressed in navy blue uniforms, wearing protective vests and baseball caps. The protective vests had two green, horizontal, high visibility stripes running across the chest. They had their pistols drawn and focused on the three bodies on the platform.

"Hey, guys, over here."

They both flinched, crouched, and pointed their pistols at me. One of them shouted something I couldn't understand.

I attempted to move my arms, hoping they realized I was zip-tied to the bench. "Please, don't shoot. I'm American," I shouted.

One of them shook his head and looked at his partner as if to say, *'It figures.'*

They left me tied to the bench for over an hour before they slapped a pair of handcuffs on and led me away. As they escorted me out through the hallway, we passed at least two dozen cops, along with the bodies of Big Tony and Lurch. We traveled through the long hall for a few minutes, passing more police, all of whom gave me the eye. They led me through to some kind of loading dock.

Outside, the sun was beginning to shine. I could see cars passing in the distance out on the street. We walked down some metal steps and into a parking lot.

With a cop on either side grasping my arm, they led me to the rear of a heavily armored white police van with blue and orange stripes. I stepped into the armored van and settled onto a metal bench. They chained my handcuffs to a steel plate welded onto the wall, closed the double doors, and a moment later we were moving. A few seconds later, the siren began to wail. There were no windows, so I couldn't look out and see where we were going. Not that it would have made any difference. I'd never been to Amsterdam before.

Forty-seven

The Amsterdam Police held me for five days and questioned me for what felt like five years. I had over six thousand euros. In cash. In my pocket. Obviously, a lot of money, but not a crime. I told them I had no idea who any of the bodies were. I lied to them and said the French guys tied me to the bench, rifled through my luggage, and stuck to my story. I never mentioned Maddie, and they never asked. I figured with close to a million bucks in her possession, she would never be found by anyone unless she wanted to be. She either disappeared in Europe, or she chartered a plane to somewhere in the world with a gorgeous beach and sunny weather. Either way, she was long gone.

The bodies of the three French guys were identified within twenty-four hours, and surprise, surprise, it turned out all three had substantial criminal records. It took a day or two longer, but Big Tony and Lurch's sordid past eventually came to light, as well. Try as they may, the Amsterdam police were at a loss to find even a shred of evidence linking me to any of the murdered individuals. Not that there was any evidence, and certainly nothing documented. Thankfully, Lurch and Big Tony were listed as residents of Minneapolis, and since my passport said I was from Saint Paul, the Amsterdam cops never saw a correlation.

I played the part of an innocent tourist ending up in the wrong place at the wrong time. In the end, with assistance, or possibly *insistence,* from the US Embassy, I was released, escorted to the airport by the Amsterdam police, and placed on a direct flight back to the states.

It was fifty minutes after four in the afternoon when we finally landed at MSP, the Minneapolis/St. Paul airport. I was so glad to be home I wanted to kiss the ground when I finally stepped off the airplane. There was a scorching sun, dreadfully high humidity, a temperature in the upper 90's. And it all felt wonderful. I ducked into the men's room for a pit stop, cleared customs, and hurried down to baggage claim.

I hadn't seen my luggage since I stepped off the train at three in the morning in Amsterdam almost a week earlier. While waiting for my suitcase to appear on carousel number two in the baggage claim I began to look forward to a shave, a long shower, and some dull days in my immediate future. No sooner had my suitcase arrived, and I pulled it off the carousel, when a voice behind me said, "Let me give you a hand with that."

I turned to look at Fat Freddy Zimmerman, flanked by two very large, very mean looking guys. He flashed a quick smile. "Welcome back, Haskell. How 'bout we give you a ride? Mr. Gustafson would like a few words with you. He's very interested in hearing all about your little trip."

"Thanks, fella's, that's very nice of you. But I was planning to just take an Uber home."

"Check that damn thing out," Fat Freddy said, indicating my suitcase.

A thug with a red lipstick smudge tattooed on his neck, yanked the suitcase out of my hand, opened it, and dumped everything out onto the floor of the baggage claim area. He ran the toe of his cowboy boot over my boxers, and my Hawaiian print shirt with the pineapples. He shook his head, tossed my suitcase against a wall, and said, "Nothing. Jack shit."

A couple of people looked at us, but wisely, no one said anything or offered to help.

"You really don't want to take an Uber, Haskell. Besides, we got a ride waiting for us right outside. At this stage, it probably would not be the best idea to disappoint Mr. Gustafson, you dumb shit." Freddy said. As we stepped out of the baggage claim area, a black SUV with tinted windows pulled up. Fat Freddy opened the passenger door and wiggled onto the front seat.

Once he was in, and the car stopped rocking, the thug with the lipstick smudge opened the back door. There were two very comfortable looking leather chairs in the back of the SUV. I started to climb in, but he placed a hand on my chest and shoved me back. "What the hell do you think you're doing? You worthless piece of shit. Wait your turn," he said and hopped in.

Once he was seated in the chair, he looked at me and growled, "Come on, get your dumb ass in here."

I began to settle into the other chair when he slapped me on the back of my head. "No way, numbnuts. You're down there, on the floor where you belong."

I looked at the area between the two seats. "I'm not gonna sit—"

This time his partner slapped me on the back of the head and said, "Get down there before we tie you to the top of the damn car."

That sounded like pretty good advice. No one said anything during the entire twenty-minute drive to the Centerfold Cabaret. We turned into the parking lot and pulled behind the back of the building next to a wooden porch and a weathered staircase leading up to the second story. Fat Freddy oozed out of his front seat and opened the door for us. The thug sitting next to the door hopped out. Lipstick Smooch, seated on the other side of me, growled, "Come on, get a move on. You're keeping the big man waiting and wasting our time."

I had to sort of crawl across the floor of the SUV to get to the door.

As Fat Freddy watched me, he shook his head. "You know, Haskell. Oh, never mind. I don't know why I'd even bother. Let's go." I followed Freddy up a rickety wooden staircase, supposedly attached to the back of the building. With Fat Freddy in the lead and the two thugs behind me, the thing wobbled and wiggled, and I was afraid it was going to collapse. Somehow, we made it up to the second story of the building without the thing falling apart. Fat Freddy unlocked a weathered wooden door and shouldered it open.

The dim hallway reeked of cheap perfume. Faded patterned wallpaper, probably from the 1950s, covered the walls. Now, large sections were missing, either torn off or simply worn away. Fat Freddy opened a door halfway down the hall and stepped inside. After an encouraging shove from Lipstick Smooch, I followed. We entered an ornate room with burgundy-colored walls, a thick oriental rug, a brass chandelier, and paintings of a partially dressed fat women that looked like they were painted in the 1890s. A large, carved, antique mahogany desk sat in front of the only window in the room. Thick burgundy colored drapery with gold fringe hung on either side of the window and was draped across the top. The drapes seemed to frame Tubby Gustafson, who was seated behind the desk in a black leather chair. He was talking on the phone. He glanced at me, and his eyes flashed a look suggesting he wanted to kill.

Fat Freddy pulled back one of the upholstered red leather chairs in front of the desk and sat down. I started to do the same, but Freddy slapped my hand off the chair and said, "What in the hell do you think you're doing? No one said you could sit down, so just wait."

Tubby finished up his phone conversation by saying, "I'm sorry, Vito. Let me call you back. I've just become aware of a problem I should have dealt with long ago. Yeah, exactly. Not to worry, I'm about to deal with that now."

Forty-eight

Tubby hung up the phone, rested his elbows on the desk, and placed his hands together as if to pray. He set his index fingers against his lips and stared at me for a long moment. He appeared deep in thought, and I had the feeling he wasn't thinking about what prayer to say for me.

"What the hell are you waiting for?" Tubby suddenly shouted. "Set your worthless ass in that chair, Haskell."

I sat down next to Fat Freddy. Tubby slowly shook his head back and forth. Eventually, he held his hands out, palms up, and softly said, "I don't know, Haskell. I just don't know. Maybe, you can tell me because, clearly, I'm in the dark. I've tried. Oh my God, how I've tried. But you seem to continue on as if you're in your own little world. Apparently, I simply don't matter. I don't know. Do I expect too much? Do I ask any more from you than I would from anyone else?"

I was about to say something when he held up his hand to silence me and said, "Please. I only have one little question." He suddenly slapped his hand on top of the desk. It sounded like a bomb going off and jiggled a crystal glass sitting on the desk and holding a quarter-inch of bourbon. He jumped to his feet and leaned forward with eyes glaring. He looked ready to kill, and he shouted, "What in the hell happened? Where is my money? Where the hell is that Maddie wench? You were supposed to watch her. Damn it." He slapped the desk again. Harder than before and this time even, Fat Freddy jumped.

I gave an audible swallow and said, "I, I don't know, sir. We were in the process of going to Amsterdam. We took a train there because these guys were following us. We stepped off the train and were about to go to the Amsterdam airport when a bunch of French guys showed up and held us at gunpoint. They were going to steal the metal briefcase Maddie said belonged to you. I tried to fight them off, but there were at least five of them, and they eventually got the better of me and knocked me out. When I came to, there were bodies scattered all around, and whoever it was must have run off with the briefcase. I guess they took your niece, Maddie, too. I tried to stop them, but there were just too many of—"

"Silencio, you moron," Tubby shouted. "Where did they go?"

"Who, sir?"

"Are you listening? These fools who took my money . . . I mean the briefcase. Where in the hell did they go?"

"I don't know, sir. Like I said, they knocked me out when I fought with them, at least five or six French guys. But I can't be sure. It might have been more. It all happened so fast. I just don't know. All I know is when I regained consciousness, they were gone, and I was chained to a metal bench. The Amsterdam cops had to use a bolt cutter to cut the chains, and then they locked me up in solitary confinement and questioned me for days on end. I didn't have a chance to look for your niece. They wouldn't let me sleep. Woke me up at all hours, played loud music, and kept calling my name over a speaker for hours on end. I became very confused. I had no idea what day it even was. The torture went on for a week straight. I just kept telling myself I had to keep my mouth shut so they wouldn't be able to tie anything to you."

Tubby straightened up and seemed to ponder what I just said. "And Maddie?"

"Your niece? I was hoping maybe you knew, sir. That's why I thought we came here to see her. Is she already studying for her bar exam?"

"No, she's not studying for her . . . She was supposed to call me every day, but she never did."

That's because those French guys seemed to be following us, and no matter what we did, they always seemed to find us. Maddie thought they might have been able to track our cell phones, so she turned her phone off and made me turn mine off, too."

"Tell me about these French bastards."

"One of them was a fat guy named Ali. He was on our plane and he—"

"How did you know his name?"

"The stewardess on the plane told me. He was seated next to me, and he was so fat they finally had to put me in another seat. I told them I wanted to stay where I was, but they insisted. Said it was some sort of safety precaution or something."

"And just why in the hell were you in Amsterdam? You had return tickets flying out of Paris. Both of you."

"That French guy and his gang kept following us around. So, I rented a car and got us out of Paris. We went to a couple of other towns, slept out in the woods for a few nights trying to hide from them. But, they always seemed to follow us. I thought since Amsterdam is a pretty big town, maybe, they had an airport, and we could get a plane back to St. Paul."

"And they kidnapped her?"

"I sure hope not, sir. I mean, that's what I think, but like I said before, I was unconscious when they took her. And, and I don't think they took her because of her money. She told me she didn't have any. So I was always paying for everything."

"You were paying for everything?" He shot a look at Fat Freddy, who quickly shrugged and shook his head no.

"Yes, sir. I was," I said, shooting an evil look Freddy's way.

"How did she hide the money?"

"The money?"

"In the suitcase, Haskell. The money that was in the damn suitcase."

"Money in the suitcase? I, I don't know, sir. I mean, I guess she would have put it in her pocket or her purse. Yeah, that's what she probably did. She put it in her purse."

Tubby stared for a long moment. "You carried her suitcase?"

"No. She wouldn't let me. She insisted on being in charge of her suitcase. In fact, she made me always get a room on a different floor from her. I think you made the room reservations for the first hotel before we even left. She had a nice suite, and I had, umm, you know, a sort of okay room. But then those French gangsters showed up. They shot someone in the hotel. I think the guy behind the front desk. I just thought it would be best if we ran away to a different hotel. Somehow, they found out which hotel we were in. After that, I rented a car, and we left Paris. I rented another car, and we left the town we went to Château-Thierry. They followed us again when we snuck off to Reims and then showed up in Amsterdam and were going to kill us. I just wanted to get her back to you safe and sound. As a matter of fact, I thought when Freddy met me at the airport, it was to come here and see Maddie."

Tubby glanced at Fat Freddy, who simply gave another shrug.

"And you don't know where she is?"

"I thought she'd be here, sir. You think she's okay? When is she scheduled to take her bar exam?"

Tubby looked at Fat Freddy and said, "Get this idiot the hell out of my sight." He was back on the phone, punching in someone's number as we hurried into the hall.

"This way," Fat Freddy said and headed in the opposite direction from where we came. That was fine with me. That wooden staircase leading up to the second story was on borrowed time.

We stepped out the front door of the Centerfold Cabaret. Nondescript music with a heavy base was playing in the barroom behind us, and some people were clapping and whistling. I tried to grab a quick glance, but all I saw was one of the brass poles and a pair of ankles swirling around it. So much for trying.

It was dusk by the time Fat Freddy kicked me out of the SUV in front of my house without so much as a good-bye. Fortunately, my house keys were in my pocket beneath the wad of euros. I opened the front door and stepped inside. Out of habit, I turned on the porch light. I was standing on two week's worth of mail, a bunch of grocery store circulars, a couple of payment due bills, and then, there was a cream-colored envelope with a familiar perfume scent and handwriting I thought I recognized. Heidi.

I opened the envelope while standing in the entry. I didn't even close the door. I pulled out a card that said 'Miss You' on the front. I opened it up and inside, in her perfect penmanship were the words, 'Sorry. Sorry. Sorry. Please, call when you get this.'

I figured she probably found some more clothes of mine or my beach towel with the message, "Say YES to Beach SEX!" I decided I'd call my office mate Louie Laufen and check on Morton instead.

Forty-nine

Louie grinned and said, "Morton? He's doing great. Although, you never mentioned he likes German beer. Not to worry, I've got a couple of cases, and I'm limiting him to just one a night."

"Morton's drinking a bottle of beer a night?"

"Yeah, I know. I know. Relax, not to worry. I put it in his water dish because he was having trouble getting it out of the bottle. Most of it was spilling on the carpet, and it kept soaking in before he could lap it up. Problem solved, once I poured it into the water dish."

I'd spent enough time at Louie's place to know Morton couldn't do any more damage to the carpeting. In fact, putting the beer in his water dish probably avoided all sorts of potentially fatal contaminations. As we continued talking, I walked out to the kitchen and opened the refrigerator. Nothing in there really caught my attention, and there were a couple of items that appeared to be way past their 'safe to eat' date.

"Took us a while to figure out the sleeping arrangements," Louie said.

"What? You mean he didn't like where you put his bed. I brought that cushion he sleeps on and—"

"Yeah, well, that didn't work. He climbed in with me. Once I gave him his own pillow, he sacked out. I think the beer helps him sleep. We get up around nine when my alarm goes off. I got him stretching his legs off over the edge of the bed. Now he doesn't wake me anymore. You know, it's been a long time since I was in bed with someone."

I didn't comment, but I had no doubt. "I was thinking I could head over and take him off your hands, Louie. I can't thank you enough for taking care of him. I can be over there in the next half hour and—"

"Naw. Don't worry about it. I got a court appearance scheduled for tomorrow at eleven. I'll bring him into the office in the morning. You two can get reacquainted and trade tales. I'm sure you're probably beat after that long flight. It'll give you a chance to unpack and catch up on your sleep."

"You sure? I mean I can head over there right now and—"

"No, don't worry about it. We're good. Besides, it's our cocktail hour." He gave a loud slurp to whatever he was drinking.

"Okay, yeah, thanks, Louie. I'll see you in the office tomorrow morning."

"See you then. Sweet dreams," Louie said and hung up.

I'd completely forgotten about my suitcase, but then other issues had taken precedence, namely Tubby Gustafson. Tubby's thug with the lipstick smooch tattoo had dumped my suitcase, and I could only hope the baggage claim folks had repacked everything.

I was about to head to the garage and drive out to the airport when the doorbell rang. I debated answering the door. Then figured I better, in case it was someone from the airport with my luggage, or worse, one of Tubby's thugs. They'd probably break a window, reach in and undo the lock.

I didn't see anyone at the door. So I unlocked it and stepped out onto the front porch. Heidi was standing at the end of the porch. Her face and hands were up against one of my front windows, and she was peering in, or at least attempting to. The window was so dirty, she couldn't possibly see anything.

"Oh, Dev. I . . . um, didn't know if you were really home. I saw your porch light on, and I didn't remember it being on all the other times I drove past, so figured I'd maybe stop and see."

"How's it going, Heidi?"

"Um, okay. You know, it could always be worse. Course it could be better, too. How have you been?"

"As well as can be expected. Just read your card. Thanks."

"I tried to give you a call, but the recording said you were unavailable. I thought maybe you forgot to pay your bill?"

"Surprisingly, no. That's not it. Actually, I was out of town. In fact, I literally just got in." I said, keeping it short. It wasn't that I was mad. Well, to tell the truth, I was more hurt than mad. Our relationship had always been off and on, almost always at her request. Right now, just seeing her gave me a lump in my throat, and I figured I had about sixty seconds left before I either started crying or screaming at her, and I didn't know which it would be.

"You want to ask me in? Maybe we could talk. You know to catch up and stuff."

"Heidi. I haven't seen you for a month and a half. Last time we saw one another, you handed me a box full of my stuff and pretty much told me to get lost."

"I didn't say that, Dev."

"Yeah, you know, I think you may be right. What you did say was you were meant to tell me about your new love. Then, you gave me the box with my tools, the paper bag with my boxers, and my St. Paul Saints sweatshirt. Fortunately, I left right away. So I didn't have to meet the stud in the red Lexus. Did he like the steaks and the wine I left?"

"Dev, please," she said. Mascara stained tears began to run down both her cheeks. "Please."

I didn't have a chance, and I knew it. "Okay, okay, come on in." We headed into the living room, and she sat down on the couch. She was sniffling, and she reached into her purse and pulled out a Kleenex. She blew her nose.

"Oh, I'm so sorry. God, look at me. I'm an absolute mess. You were right, Dev. I'm just a stupid bitch."

"Heidi, I never said that."

"No, but I know you were thinking it." I didn't argue. "Turned out, Josh was going through a divorce, and he and his bitchy wife ended up getting back together. Serves them both right. They deserve one another," she said and blew her nose again.

I knew I didn't have a snowball's chance in hell. "Would you like a glass of wine?"

"Well, maybe. If that would be okay with you."

"Yeah, it would be more than okay. It's great to see you."

"Really?" She sniffled and wiped her nose with the Kleenex.

"Yeah. I missed you. A lot."

She exhaled, and I could sense the stress beginning to depart. "Thanks. If you just got home, have you had any dinner?"

"Not yet. I just made a phone call to Louie to go pick up Morton, but he wants to keep him for another night. And then you rang the doorbell just as I hung up."

"Let me go get some takeout, and we can have dinner."

"You haven't eaten?"

"No, I've been out of sorts ever since loser Josh dumped me. At least I lost five pounds, but suddenly, I'm famished." She pulled her phone out and speed-dialed a number. She ordered two shrimp pasta's and hung up. "They'll be ready in fifteen minutes. That will give you time to jump in the shower and get cleaned up while

I go get them." She was already returning to the Heidi I knew.

Fifty

I decided I could probably go to the airport tomorrow morning to see if they still had my luggage. So I quickly showered, shaved, and put on the cleanest clothes I could find. I tossed the moldy cheese, rotted lettuce, and spoiled milk in the trash and ran all of it out to the bin. I set the kitchen counter with placemats and wine glasses. I dimmed the lights and put on some soft music. I charged out to the backyard again and cut a bunch of my neighbor's daises that were hanging over into my yard. I had just finished arranging them in a beer mug when the doorbell rang.

Heidi was standing at the front door. I opened the door, and she said, "Looks like you got a delivery." A large box sat in the middle of the doorway.

"It must have come while I was in the shower."

She stepped over it, gave me a long kiss and said, "I'll put this stuff in the kitchen if you want to grab that box. It looks heavy."

I watched until she strutted out of sight before I picked up the box. She was right. It was heavy. I picked it up and followed her into the kitchen. She pulled two white styrofoam trays from the paper bag along with a bottle of red wine.

"What did you order?" She said.

"I haven't ordered anything. I have no idea what this could be." I didn't recognize the handwriting on the label. I noticed the return address on the shipping label. The package was from France. Château-Thierry, to be exact.

"Well, aren't you going to open it?"

"Huh? Oh, yeah, I suppose I better." I pulled a knife from the rack, slit the tape, and opened the box. Twelve bottles with the tops wrapped in white foil starred back at me. Each bottle was surrounded by a sleeve of bubble wrap. "What the . . ." I lifted one of the bottles and pulled off the bubble wrap. The bottle was brown and flared out slightly before forming a long neck. The label read;

CHAMPAIGN

PANNIER

Blanc

Velours

"Are you kidding me? You bought a case of Champagne online and had it shipped all the way from France? Since when did you start liking this stuff?" Heidi said.

"I didn't buy it. It was a nice place and all, but I'm still not a big fan of Champagne."

"What do you mean, it was a nice place? You were there? In France? You?"

"Yeah, little more than a week ago."

Heidi peeked in the box and pulled out a piece of paper. She unfolded it and got a funny look on her face. "You must have done something right. They sent you this note." She handed me the sheet of paper. Handwritten across the sheet of paper were the words,

"THANK YOU"

M

"Oh, man. She must have made it," I said more to myself.

"What? You met a woman who makes Champagne?"

"No. She's going to be a teacher. You want a glass?"

"Maybe chill one of those bottles for later on. We've got all night," Heidi said and kissed me.

The End

Thank you for reading **International Incident**. If you enjoyed the read please consider leaving a review. It really, really helps. Thanks in advance.

Don't miss the sample of **Guest From Hell**, the next work of genius in the Dev Haskell series.

Guest From Hell

Second Edition

MIKE FARICY

Prologue

It wasn't quite dusk on the humid night they suddenly appeared at the side of the cabin and headed for the dock. Cabin was a colloquial term. Yes, it was on a lake, all three stories, but it had central air, internet, a designer kitchen, a theatre room, six bedrooms all en suite, and almost a million dollars' worth of oil paintings hanging on the walls. Sheldon Smeet was out on his dock sipping bourbon and admiring the cigar boat he'd purchased last spring. It was a gorgeous thing that, unfortunately, had been tied to the dock since the day it arrived three months ago.

Thankfully his visitor had left. As wonderful as the sex was after her vodkas and his promise to correct the eviction papers, he was glad to see her head down the road in her red Audi. He sipped the expensive bourbon and admired the cut crystal glass, almost two hundred years old with an Irish harp cut in the center. He was enjoying the peace and quiet, unaware anyone else was around until he heard the heavy footsteps on the metal dock. There were four of them. Of course, by then it was too late, nowhere to run, and he couldn't swim. He caught his breath and took a sip from the crystal glass to steady himself.

"Sheldon. Thought we might find you down here. Wondered if you'd come to a decision on our offer. I think we've been more than patient. It's been two weeks, and we told you we needed an answer right away."

"With everything that's been going on, I've turned that over to my major investor. His team is examining the offer and—"

"Sheldon, Sheldon, Sheldon. We've had this conversation before. The way you've set things up, you have the final say. I think it would be nice if you gave the go-ahead, now."

"It's being examined, and we're in the process of weighing options. It shouldn't be too long," he said and drained his glass.

"I see, I see. Okay, fair enough. Now, is this yours?" He nodded toward the cigar boat. "It looks fast."

"Yes, I um, actually haven't had the opportunity to use it. But it's supposed to be very fast."

"Haven't used it? Why not?"

"Actually, I don't know how. I'll need someone to chauffeur me around. I know, it sounds crazy, but that's the case."

"Don't know how to drive it. That can't be much fun. Tell you what, Liam here, he grew up on a large island. I'll bet he knows how to drive this thing. Liam, you think you could start this baby up?"

"No problem, boss."

"Oh, listen, thanks fellows, but really, you don't need to—"

"Nonsense, Liam, fire this puppy up."

"No really," Sheldon said as Liam hopped over the side and settled into the captain's chair. A moment later, the engine started, and the water began churning at the rear of the boat.

"See? There you go, Sheldon. All set. You sure you don't want to sign that paperwork right now? I brought a copy. We can get your signature right here." He snapped his fingers at one of the men behind him, and he was handed a pen. "What do you say, Sheldon. You ready to sign?"

"Hey, come on now. I told you my partners are going over the paperwork. I'll have an answer for you in the next day or two, and then we—"

"I don't think you're listening, Sheldon. I don't want to wait a day or two. You get the woman out of the place. We do the deal, and everything works out for the best."

"I told you I can't. I have to wait for my partners to review—"

"Yeah, I guess you did tell me that. Let me ask you something, Sheldon. You left or right-handed?"

"What? Um, left-handed. What does that have to do with anything?"

"One more chance, Sheldon. Will you sign the documents? I'm even adding a please. Please sign the documents."

"All right, I've heard just about enough. I want you out of here and off my property immediately. Do you hear me? Immediately or I'm calling the police."

The man shook his head and said, "Bad move, Sheldon. Tell you what. Let me hold that glass, it looks expensive."

"Looks expensive? Now, I want all of you out of here immediately."

The large man nodded, half-turned, and suddenly stomped on Sheldon's foot. As Sheldon screamed and bent forward, the man grabbed the crystal glass. "Damn it, Sheldon. I warned you, but you wouldn't listen. Okay fellas, get on with it."

The two men suddenly grabbed Sheldon and forced him to his knees. The larger of the two pushed him down, placing his knee in the small of Sheldon's back while the other man took hold of Sheldon's right arm and pulled it toward the prop on the large outboard engine.

"No, no, no," Sheldon shouted and then screamed.

One

Heidi had been treating me like a king ever since she picked me up. "No, Dev. You're always doing such nice things for me. You are not buying dinner. I'm paying. Was there anything else you wanted? Another drink? More dessert?"

I was enjoying myself. She'd made reservations at the Saint Paul Grill, a top-notch place that I loved. She didn't say a thing when she picked me up. Usually, I heard something like, 'That's what you're wearing?' But not tonight. I ordered a rare steak and no vegetable, she just smiled, leaned over, and gave me a kiss. She smiled when I ordered dessert, apple crisp with cinnamon ice cream. On any other night, she'd skip dessert then eat two-thirds of mine. Tonight, she only took one little spoonful when it was set in front of me. To be honest, she was acting so nice I wondered what was up.

When we stepped out of the restaurant, she said, "You feel like going anywhere? Or, if you want, we could just head back to your place. I'm dying to give you a back rub."

"Heidi, what's going on? You've been so nice tonight. I don't think I've ever seen you like this before."

She laughed. "Oh Dev, sometimes . . . What, I can't try to please the one man I adore? I know, why don't we head over to The Spot. We can grab a drink, get you in the frame of mind for some late-night romance. You can think about all the different things you might like to do later on."

"That part certainly sounds fun. But, The Spot? Didn't you tell me to never, ever mention the place in your presence? You make me take a shower after I've been there, so you don't contract any germs."

"Mmm-mmm, you're such a sweetie," she said, pinching my cheek almost too hard. I was just about ready to scream when she let go and gave me a kiss. "I don't know. I may not be able to wait. Maybe we should just climb into the back seat of my car. Want to?" she said and flashed her eyes.

"But just a minute ago you wanted to go to The Spot?"

"Are you kidding? The opportunity to go to The Spot with my stud-muffin? Let's do it. I can show you off and lay claim to you in front of all those wenches who are always hitting on you."

"You're talking about The Spot, right? The bar just across from my office?"

"Yeah, where else? Let's go there, but we're only staying for one. I want to get back to your place and have you all to myself. I've got plans for you tonight, mister. I hope you've rested up."

"Yeah. Let's go for one."

Heidi climbed in behind the wheel, leaned over, and gave me a big kiss then headed toward The Spot. She softly rubbed my inner thigh the entire way there. I got another big kiss once she pulled alongside the place.

"Mmm-mmm, let's not take too long, Dev. You've got me all worked up. God, I'm ready to eat you alive. Grrr-Grrr," she said then laughed and climbed out of the car. We headed in the side door. The place was maybe half-full, but then it was barely nine. Heads turned when we walked in. Heidi had been in before, but she hadn't darkened the doorway in at least three or four years. The last time she was here, a guy was standing naked at the corner of the bar, drinking a beer. I mentioned it to Jimmy the bartender that night. 'Well, yeah, it's his birthday' he'd said, suggesting it was okay because the guy was in his birthday suit. Heidi had waited for me out in the car and vowed she'd never, ever set foot in there again.

So now, here she was, prancing through The Spot, walking as if she was on a fashion runway. She placed one foot directly in front of the other, shaking her attributes. As she strutted past, every male in the place focused on her. Her short, very tight skirt displayed the hint of an extremely small thong on her rear. I knew one of the guys, and just as I said, "Hi Timmy," his wife hit him on the shoulder to get his attention back.

Heidi pranced up to the bar as two ne'er-do-wells smiled and made room for her between them.

Mike was bartending tonight. "If you don't mind me saying, you look like the sort of woman who could do a lot better than Dev Haskell."

Heidi gave a little laugh and said, "You kidding? He's way more than I can handle."

Shocked looks fell across every face within hearing distance.

"What'll it be, ma'am?"

"I think just a glass of wine for me."

"Red or white?"

She didn't blink. "The red would be perfect."

"The usual, Dev?"

"Yeah, thanks, Mike."

I started to take my wallet out as Mike placed a glass beneath the Summit IPA tap. Heidi placed her hand on my arm. "No, darling. I'm getting this."

"But you bought dinner."

"And now I'm buying you an after-dinner drink. You sure you wouldn't like a bourbon or an Irish whiskey?"

"No, thanks, the beer is just fine."

Mike placed an empty wine glass and an airline bottle of red wine on the bar. "Eight dollars, even," he said.

Heidi slid a ten across the bar, smiled, and said, "Keep the change."

"I don't know, Dev. Such a nice woman and she ends up with you. Thank you, ma'am. Just a warning, you've got a lot of work to do," he said and nodded at me.

TWO

Morton met us at the front door. He was a big fan of Heidi's. He'd already chewed up at least a dozen of her thongs. As she stepped into the front entry, she gave him a healthy rub behind his ears and said, "Oh Morton. How are you? Have you been a good boy? Have you? Oh, good boy, Morton. Good boy."

Morton's tail was wagging back and forth, slamming against the open door and then the wall.

"Give me just a minute while I let him out back," I said. "Come on, Morton. Come on."

He'd just shoved his nose between Heidi's thighs and didn't appear to be interested in going anywhere at the moment.

"Morton. Come on, outside. Morton. Outside. Come on. Let's go."

"Apparently, he's not listening to you, Dev."

"Who can blame him?"

"Come on, Morton. Outside. Treat, Morton. Come on. You want a treat? Come on, Morton."

His tail continued to slap against the wall.

Heidi gave him another rub behind the ears and then said, "Come on, Morton. Let's go outside. You've been stuck in the house for a couple of hours. Come on, Morton. Let's go." Heidi pushed his nose away from her thighs and headed for the back door. Morton followed in hot pursuit, ignoring me completely. Heidi opened the back door and stepped out onto the porch. There was a worn green tennis ball in the middle of the porch, and she kicked it into the backyard. Morton bounded off the porch after the ball. They were back inside after a couple of minutes.

"Can I pour you a whiskey or something before we go upstairs?" she asked, raising her eyebrows.

"Yeah, a little whiskey might be good. I'm pouring, so don't even suggest. You've done way more than your fair share tonight. I've been nothing but a complete load the entire evening. Now it's my turn to wait on you."

"Dev darling, I just want to show you how special you are."

"Heidi, by and large, you've always been good to me. And I hope you view me in the same light. But tonight was over the top. I got the feeling you would have brushed my teeth for me if I asked you."

"Dev, can't I be nice to you and you just accept it? You don't have to question it. I love being kind, and grateful, and loving, and compassionate, and—"

"Not to worry, Heidi. You're all those things and more. Really you are, but tonight, I mean, wow."

"Maybe you should get used to it. I tell you what. Since you want to do something for me, why don't you pour me a glass of wine and I'm just going to slip into something a little more comfortable. Okay?"

"Okay. I'll be up in a couple of minutes."

She headed for the stairs with Morton following close behind.

"Morton, treat," I called and rattled the lid to the cookie jar where I kept the dog biscuits. He stopped and looked then glanced at Heidi climbing up the staircase. He seemed to ponder the alternatives for a long moment then hurried back into the kitchen, tail wagging, for the sure thing.

Three

I took my time filling Heidi's wine glass and my glass of whiskey. When I brought them up to the bedroom, Heidi was in bed leaning up against the headboard. The overhead light was off and just the lamp on the end table next to her was on. She was wearing a very small, black lace affair that didn't even begin to cover. I'd seen church veils that were larger. It was gorgeous.

I stood in the doorway, staring.

"Oh, you like?"

"It's gorgeous. I don't think I've ever seen it before."

"I know you haven't. I thought you might like it. I got it especially for tonight."

"Oh man, that is one sexy little number." I hurried around to the far side of the bed and set her wine glass on the table next to the lamp. I ran back around the bed, set my whiskey glass down, and quickly kicked off my shoes. I pulled my trousers off and tossed them on the floor.

"Oh Dev, you are getting me so hot. Get in here. Hurry up, I really need you."

I started to unbutton my shirt. The second button seemed to be stuck somehow, and I pulled on the shirt, four buttons flew off and bounced against the wall. Not that I cared. I let the shirt drop onto the floor and climbed into the bed.

"Oh, much better," Heidi said and tossed her little lace affair onto my head.

"Heidi, this has been the most wonderful night we've had in a long time, maybe even ever."

She pushed me down onto the pillow then hopped on top of me. "And it's not over yet. You just never realized how absolutely infatuated I am with you, Dev. It's all I can do to keep my hands off of you."

"Well, don't worry about that now. Please, help yourself."

"Oh, I intend to," she said, She ducked beneath the sheet and began to slide down my chest. She had just finished kissing my navel, and I was thinking, *'Oh this is going to be so good.'* When suddenly, she popped her head up and said, "Hey, I don't know if I should even ask you this, but, well, I have a friend who could maybe use some help. I was just wondering if you'd consider talking to her and seeing what you might be able to do for her."

"A, a friend?" It suddenly wasn't making sense at the moment. "Maybe we could discuss this a little later. You were just about to—"

"Oh, yeah, sure. But see, well, she's out of time." She suddenly climbed off me and leaned back against the headboard. She took a deep breath and exhaled as if she'd just run some gauntlet and made it safely to the other side. She grabbed her glass of wine, took a sip, and then held it in front of her as if it were some force shield that would keep me at bay.

"So here's the deal. I've known Roxanne LaRue, I call her Roxy, I've known her since kindergarten. It's where we met."

"Maybe we could get back to the matters at hand, Heidi, and discuss this over breakfast."

"Relax, this'll just take a minute. So, like I was saying, we met in kindergarten and became fast friends on the first day. We always picked one another for our teams. We jumped rope, played Barbies, went to the same high school. Both of us went to the U, but she dropped out after a couple of years and started her career as a professional dancer."

"Professional dancer?"

"Yeah, that's right. Anyway, things didn't work out. To make a long story short, she bought a house on the night before the 2008 recession hit. Of course, the property value dropped by fifty percent. The bank called the loan. She borrowed from another firm and has kind of been dodging ever since."

"Dodging," I said and took a sip of my whiskey.

"Yeah, like I said, it hasn't worked out the best for her. Anyway, now she's going to be evicted. Some rough guys served her notice, threatened her, and she's supposed to be out of her place by next week."

"Next week? How long has this been going on? Usually, she'd have to be in arrears for some time, maybe six months or so."

"Well, that might have been the case. I'm not exactly sure. But these really rough guys, two of them, served her with the notice and told her she only had a week to get all her stuff out of there."

"A week? And she was just served?"

"Yeah," she said and took a sip of wine. "If you could maybe talk to her because the way she was served doesn't seem to make any sense to me."

"Yeah, I suppose I could. But you're the financial wizard. Have you checked this out?"

"You mean her being in arrears? Yeah, that part is legit, although the interest rate she was paying is ten point five. That's more than double the national average. Right now, it's about four point two."

"Double the national average? What bank did she go through?"

"Third National."

"Third National? Aren't they the ones having all sorts of problems? They're under some sort of investigation right now, aren't they?"

"As a matter of fact, they're under a number of investigations, and Roxy's been involved in some of that."

"Involved?"

"Yeah, she um, maybe had a bit of a personal relationship that facilitated getting the mortgage, and well, the feds are in the process of checking that out. Now the bank wants to get her off the books as fast as possible."

"She isn't one of the women supposedly associated with the bank president, what's his name, is she?"

"His name is Sheldon Smeet, a real jerk. And to answer your questions, yes. She more or less earned the mortgage, if that translates."

"Meaning she probably wasn't qualified to begin with."

"Certainly not for the amount she was given. I mean, if the house had been available for say two hundred thousand, yeah she maybe would have been qualified, if she could have held onto her job."

"So, what happened? She got fired or quit and couldn't make the payments?"

"That's part of it. The other part is that she was in way over her head. The property was appraised at nine-seventy-five and—"

"Nine-seventy-five as in nine hundred and seventy-five thousand dollars?"

"Yeah, and she actually ended up paying a million two."

"What?"

"Yeah, she's got a bit of a problem."

"But they financed her?"

"Well, between her relationship with Sheldon Smeet and his basically bypassing all the standard loan provisions and signing off on her loan, yeah, they financed her. Financed her at ten point five percent."

"Heidi, what am I supposed to do?"

"Well, you know certain people. Certain types of people, and I was just thinking if you could maybe get these scary guys to back off. You know."

"Actually, no, I don't know."

"Could you at least talk to her and maybe hear her side of the story?"

"Her side? Does she even know it?"

"Well, yeah, there is that. But maybe if you talked with her, you know."

"Okay, yeah sure, Heidi. I'll talk to her. Thanks for thinking of me. Since she's a friend of yours, I'll see what I can do. Now, where were we before you brought up your friend Roxy?"

"Oh, thank you, Dev. Thanks so much. If you just talk to her, I know it may be mission impossible, but if you could at least take a look. It's just that I've known her since we were little girls, and everything that's gone wrong has been due to her own bad decisions. I know all that. But she's still my oldest friend."

"Okay, for you, I'll do it."

"Oh, thanks," she said and drained her glass of wine. "I've been agonizing over this ever since I learned the news. God, I feel like a giant weight has been lifted off my shoulders. Honest to God, I mean, I feel exhausted. You mind if we just go to sleep?"

Four

ouie shook his head. "So what? You're going to go over the paperwork on the loan?"

Louie Laufen, attorney. Also known as ***the*** attorney to represent you in the Ramsey County court system when you've been charged with a DUI, Driving While Intoxicated. He's also my officemate. When he asked if I was going to go over the paperwork, he said it in a tone that suggested, *'What idiot thought this up.?* Since numbers and paperwork are not exactly my strong suit.

"No, that's not what I plan to do. Apparently, there are a couple of rough guys who want her out of the house within the week. That sounds a little rushed to me, and then theoretically, she would still be liable for whatever the loan is. By the way, the loan is at ten point two percent."

"Ten point two? That's nuts."

"You think? Just the little I've learned checking out this Sheldon Smeet guy on Google, he's a real piece of work."

"I'm always reminded of the words a wise man told me years ago," Louie said. "You got the Feds on your ass. They already got you. At that point, it's just a matter of time before they decide to snap the trap."

"I don't know. Maybe she can plead stupid or offer assistance to the Feds or something. Sounds like she doesn't have the money and maybe never will. But if she could hang onto and sell the place, maybe she could knock down that payment due amount."

"It all seems like a pretty tall order."

"Well, first things first. Maybe I try to get the thugs off her back. Then take it from there."

"Do you have a plan for the thugs?" Louie said.

"As a matter of fact, I do."

Five

The following morning, I was in the process of putting the first part of my plan to work. I was meeting Roxanne LaRue for lunch over at The Burger Bitches. It was a little burger joint with a couple of booths against the far wall that would be nice and private. The place sits on a corner just across the street from the old railroad station downtown. It's about fifteen feet wide with a 50s vintage luncheon counter and is run by a woman I know named Siobhan. She was a former professional dancer, think stripper, who did five years in Minnesota's only state prison for women, located in the town of Shakopee. The railroad station had been turned into condos a few years back and gave Siobhan an almost built-in clientele. Not that she needed it. She does up a mean burger, has won all sorts of awards, and there's a line out the door every day for two hours over the noon hour. The staff is all female. It's one of those places where guys in suits and motorcycle colors mingle, and there are never any problems. I got there early just to be sure I could score one of the booths on the far wall.

"I don't believe it, Dev Haskell? Long time no see, baby."

"Hey Siobhan, yeah, long time no see. How's it go-ing?"

"Working my ass off."

Quite an accomplishment. She'd put on about sixty pounds since the last time I saw her. Apparently, she still had a lot more to work off.

"You getting something to go, or do you intend to grace us with your presence today?" she said.

"Actually, meeting someone down here. Friend of a friend. Would it be okay if I grabbed one of the booths? We might be there awhile."

"You're good but better grab it now, they fill up quick. What can I get you?"

"Maybe just a glass of water while I wait."

"Bad idea, Dev. Everyone'll be giving you the evil eye wondering when you're gonna get your ass out of there. Connie," she yelled, "do up a strawberry malt and bring it to this degenerate looking guy in the St. Paul Saints jersey. He'll be wasting his time and taking up space in the back booth."

"Thanks, Siobhan."

"You don't know what I'm gonna charge you, sweetheart."

"Just be nice."

Forty-five minutes later, I was just about finished with the strawberry malt and was checking my cellphone for the umpteenth time when a sexy voice said, "You must be Dev Haskell. Heidi's told me all about you."

I looked up as Roxy leaned down and gave me a kiss on the forehead. She was wearing a too-small t-shirt that was stretched to the limit and cutoff jeans that were so short the pockets hung down an inch or two below the jeans.

"No, my name's Bill but sit down anyway."

She didn't look at all flustered. Instead, she said, "Oh, sorry, I'd love to join you, but I have to meet a guy. Maybe we could get together some other time?"

"Just kidding, you must be Roxy."

"Oh. Yeah, Heidi was right. You're a piece of work," she said, sliding in across from me. "Nice to meet you, Dev."

"Likewise. Heidi said you two go back quite a ways."

"Yeah, little kids on the first day of school and we quickly became best of friends. She was always the studious one. I'm still the party animal. What's that you're drinking?"

"Strawberry malt. I highly recommend it."

The noon rush was in full swing, and the crowd was two deep all along the lunch counter. Everyone was waving cash as they waited for their orders to be filled. The place smelled of cheeseburgers, fries, and onion rings.

"They have a bar?" she said, looking around.

"A bar? No, they don't. The place is run by a friend of mine. She did some time, got out, and started this place. With her record, she was never going to get a liquor license. Plus, she hires other women just out on parole trying to work their way back into society, so strawberry malts are about as good as it's gonna get."

"I guess I could try one."

I saw Siobhan staring at us through the crowd, studying Roxy. I pointed at my nearly empty malt and pointed at Roxy. Siobhan nodded and gave me the thumbs-up.

"So Heidi didn't tell me much, other than you've been dealing with some mortgage problems and I guess you got served with an eviction notice."

She shrugged and said, "Yeah, a couple of jerks. They're going to be back tomorrow at eleven. Said I have to be out or they're gonna throw me out."

"Do you have the funds to bring your loan current?"

"Hello. If I had the money, we wouldn't be sitting here. Hell, if I had the money, I wouldn't have done that worthless dip shit, Sheldon Smeet. Talk about a lousy screw, and now he's come back and is really screwing me."

I was quickly arriving at the conclusion that, other than buying lunch for Roxy, there was nothing I could do to help her. "I understand you've been interviewed by the Feds. Did they ask you about the loan procedure?"

"The loan procedure?" she scoffed. "You kidding? Sheldon and I had a three-day meeting in a hotel room in Las Vegas where I drank martinis, wore a smile, and pretended Sheldon was the best thing since sliced bread. After that, I signed a couple pieces of paper, and he handed me the keys on the plane ride home."

"And you got a loan for a million two?"

"Yeah, I guess. At least on paper. But he never said anything about a loan. It's not like I ever saw any money. I mean he had this cool place, and I got to move in. He would stop by a couple of times a week, always called to make sure no one else was there before he showed up. I mean, it was all working great as far as I was concerned. Then all of a sudden these two big, hairy guys show up, tell me I have to be out of there in less than a week and oh, by the way, I owe Sheldon's bank over a million bucks. A million bucks? I could be dancing from now till doomsday, and I'd never see a million bucks."

Siobhan suddenly appeared with a strawberry malt and set it down in front of Roxy. "Here you go. Say, don't I know you from somewhere?" she said, studying Roxy.

Roxy looked up and said, "Cherry?"

"That was a few years back, honey. And you were, no wait, don't tell me. You're, yeah, you're Kitten. Right?"

Roxy laughed and said, "Yeah, that was the name I used then. Now I just go by my real name, Roxy."

"You still dancing?"

"Not exactly. I'm more into the ah, private client thingy. You know, hanging on some rich guy's arm, making him look successful."

"That working out for you?"

"Sometimes," Roxy said. She took a long pull on the straw standing in the strawberry malt, suggesting the conversation was over.

"Well, you ever need a part-time gig, let me know. We open at eleven and close at three."

"Thanks, but I'm doing just fine."

"Yeah, I'm sure you are. I'll leave you to it. Nice seeing you, Kitten," Siobhan said. She gave me a nod and stepped away. The crowd automatically made a wide path for her as she headed back behind the lunch counter.

We talked for another twenty minutes, not that I really learned anything. Roxy took a final sip of her malt. It was barely half-empty. "You interested in seeing the place?"

"I guess I could take a look. You got the time?"

"Nothing scheduled. I'm parked around the corner. I'm in a red Audi. Why don't you follow me?"

I left a ten-dollar bill on the table and headed out the door. I gave Siobhan a wave as I left, and she pointed her index finger and thumb at me in the shape of a gun and fired then shook her head back and forth as if suggesting I'd never learn.

To be continued...

Roxy? Siobhan? A million dollars? And just where does Sheldon Smeet and his bank fit into all this? Better click on the link and grab your copy of **<u>Guest From Hell</u>**, to find out exactly what's going on.

Books by Mike Faricy
Crime Fiction Firsts

A boxset of the first four books in four crime fiction series:

Russian Roulette; Dev Haskell series
Welcome; Jack Dillon Dublin Tales series
Corridor Man; Corridor Man series
Reduced Ransom! Hot Shot series

The following titles comprise the Dev Haskell series:

Russian Roulette: Case 1
Mr. Swirlee: Case 2
Bite Me: Case 3
Bombshell: Case 4
Tutti Frutti: Case 5
Last Shot: Case 6
Ting-A-Ling: Case 7
Crickett: Case 8
Bulldog: Case 9
Double Trouble: Case 10
Yellow Ribbon: Case 11
Dog Gone: Case 12
Scam Man: Case 13
Foiled: Case 14
What Happens in Vegas… Case 15
Art Hound: Case 16
The Office: Case 17

Star Struck: Case 18
International Incident: Case 19
Guest From Hell: Case 20
Art Attack: Case 21
Mystery Man: Case 22
Bow-Wow Rescue: Case 23
Cold Case: Case 24
Cash Up Front: Case 25
Dream House: Case 26
Alley Katz: Case 27
The Big Gamble: Case 28
Bad to the Bone: Case 29
Silencio!: Case 30
Surprise, Surprise: Case 31
Hit & Run: Case 32
Suspect Santa: Case 33
P.I. Apprentice: Case 34
Rebel Without a Clue: Case 35

The following titles are Dev Haskell novellas:
Dollhouse
The Dance
Pixie
Fore!
Twinkle Toes
(*a Dev Haskell short story*)

The following are Dev Haskell Boxsets:
Dev Haskell Boxset 1-3
Dev Haskell Boxset 4-6
Dev Haskell Boxset 7-9
Dev Haskell Boxset 10-12
Dev Haskell Boxset 13-15
Dev Haskell Boxset 16-18
Dev Haskell Boxset 19-21
Dev Haskell Boxset 22-24
Dev Haskell Boxset 25-27
Dev Haskell Boxset 28-30
Dev Haskell Boxset 1-7
Dev Haskell Boxset 8-14
Dev Haskell Boxset 15-19
Dev Haskell Boxset 20-24
Dev Haskell Boxset 25-29

The following titles comprise the Jack Dillon Dublin Tales series:
Welcome
Jack Dillon Dublin Tale 1
Sweet Dreams
Jack Dillon Dublin Tale 2
Mirror Mirror
Jack Dillon Dublin Tale 3
Silver Bullet
Jack Dillon Dublin Tale 4
Fair City Blues
Jack Dillon Dublin Tale 5

Spade Work
Jack Dillon Dublin Tale 6
Madeline Missing
Jack Dillon Dublin Tale 7
Mistaken Identity
Jack Dillon Dublin Tale 8
Picture Perfect
Jack Dillon Dublin Tale 9
Dublin Moon
Jack Dillon Dublin Tale 10
Mystery Woman
Jack Dillon Dublin Tale 11
Second Chance
Jack Dillon Dublin Tale 12
Payback Brother
Jack Dillon Dublin Tale 13
The Heist
Jack Dillon Dublin Tale 14
Jewels To Kill For
Jack Dillon Dublin Tale 15
Retirement Scheme
Jack Dillon Dublin Tale 16
The Collector
Jack Dillon Dublin Tale 17

Jack Dillon Dublin Tales Boxsets:
Jack Dillon Dublin Tales 1-3
Jack Dillon Dublin Tales 4-6
Jack Dillon Dublin Tales 1-5

Jack Dillon Dublin Tales 1-7
Jack Dillon Dublin Tales 6-10

The following titles comprise the Hotshot series;
Reduced Ransom! Second Edition
Finders Keepers! Second Edition
Bankers Hours Second Edition
Chow Down Second Edition
Moonlight Dance Academy Second Edition
Irish Dukes (Fight Card Series)
written under the pseudonym Jack Tunney

The following titles comprise the Corridor Man series:
Corridor Man
Corridor Man 2: Opportunity knocks
Corridor Man 3: The Dungeon
Corridor Man 4: Dead End
Corridor Man 5: Finger
Corridor Man 6: Exit Strategy
Corridor Man 7: Trunk Music
Corridor Man 8: Birthday Boy
Corridor Man 9: Boss Man
Corridor Man 10: Bye Bye Bobby

Corridor Man novellas:
Corridor Man: Valentine
Corridor Man: Auditor
Corridor Man: Howling

Corridor Man: Spa Day

The following are Corridor Man Boxsets:
Corridor Man Boxset 1-3
Corridor Man Boxset 1-5
Corridor Man Boxset 6-9

All books are available on Amazon.com

Thank you!

Contact the author:
- Email: mikefaricyauthor@gmail.com
- Twitter: @Mikefaricybooks
- Facebook: Mike Faricy Author
- Website: http://www.mikefaricybooks.com

Published by

MJF Publishing